(

Turning out the office light for the evening, Sarah was finally heading home. She was exhausted after meeting with disgruntled clients all afternoon. The threats made by John Archer were particularly disturbing. Archer was involved in a nasty divorce and custody battle and was furious at the thought of giving his soon-to-be ex-wife, Jill, one red cent of his fortune. Never mind that she had been a faithful wife, as well as the mother of his two sons, Jason and Brandon. The bottom line was that Archer didn't want the divorce. Jill, however, was adamant about ending the marriage. She also wanted the house and custody of the children. As her attorney, it was Sarah's job to make sure she received everything she wanted and more.

John Archer was a self-made millionaire who had no chance of being nominated for father of the year. He displayed little or no interest in his children, but chose to fight for custody simply because he hated to lose at anything. Archer was the proverbial control freak. He viewed his wife and kids as personal property; his by right of attainment. Fortunately Jason was approaching legal age, and had chosen to live with his mother. Brandon was a couple of years younger, but was always closer to his mother and, with Jason choosing mom, Brandon followed his brother, as usual. The law in this State mandates equal distribution of marital property. Jill wanted to keep the house on Lexington which, for the children and her, had always been their primary place of residence. It was the largest of the Archers four estates. The total family worth was still being calculated. Just yesterday, Sarah requested full disclosure of all marital assets including all corporate financial holdings.

Expecting to hear from Archer's attorney, Sarah was stunned when she received a call from Archer himself. The voice on the phone was deep and husky. Archer made his displeasure known, telling Sarah exactly what he thought of her prying into his financial affairs. His tone resonated with unsuppressed anger. Sarah had no intention of enduring Archer's verbal abuse and advised him that he should direct his complaints to his own attorney. Archer became even more incensed, telling Sarah that little girls like her were safer on their own side of the playground. Sarah could not believe the man's gall. She had dealt many times with men like him, and refused to be intimidated. Sarah chuckled lightly as she told Archer precisely what she thought of his opinions. Enraged, Archer yelled that by the time he was through, both she and his wife would get exactly what they deserved. The sound of a dial tone buzzing in her ear gave notice that Archer had ended the conversation. Days like today made Sarah think seriously about giving up her legal career.

Sarah closed her office door and headed down the hallway to the elevator. Most of the staff had already left for the day. The corridor was dim. The exit light above the elevator provided the only real light in the hallway. Sarah had walked past several closed doors when she noticed that the one just ahead of her on the right was still open. There was light coming from this office. Not all the lights were on - maybe a desk lamp. It was Thornton Hilliard's office. Thornton worked in the firm's Intellectual Property section.

As she approached Thornton's office, she could hear him in a heated conversation. He was shouting that he couldn't do whatever it was that the person on the other end of the phone wanted him to do, and that he had gone way too far as it was. Sarah slowed as she neared the door. She noticed a shadow… moving. It was Thornton. He was pacing in front of the desk as he spoke, no shouted, into the phone. She peered in to get a closer look. She could see Thornton pacing. Just as she was about to make herself known, he walked over and slammed the door shut. Sarah was so startled that she dropped her purse. Bending to retrieve it, she quickly picked up the fallen contents and proceeded to the elevator, stopping to look back at the now closed office door. Arriving downstairs, she signed out, said goodnight to Chester the security guard, and headed to her car.

Sarah started the car. An old Frank Sinatra tune began playing on the radio. Nothing was more relaxing after a long hard day than listening to old blue eyes sing his way into your heart. Why did life have to be so complicated? The plan was to spend seven years busting her butt at the firm, make partner, ten more years of hard work, then coast down easy street. Eight long and grueling years later she was still searching for the elusive partnership. Stopping at a red light, Sarah closed her eyes, laid her head against the steering wheel and contemplated how she had gotten to this place in her life. She was a long distance runner in college, an Olympic hopeful with dreams of some day traveling the world. Unfortunately, her dreams were destroyed by an unexpected accident. She had blown out her knee. There was no apparent reason for the freak injury. She was reaching her stride. Left foot, right foot, left foot, and BAM! The right knee simply gave out. The energy that she once applied to running was swiftly transferred to her law school studies. Graduating in the top three percent of her class from Stanford, she was aggressively pursued by the firm.

Now, as she sat at the light, eight years later, she wondered whether the firm's pursuit of her was simply to fill a quota, and whether she would ever make partner. Sure, promises were made, but those promises never seemed to materialize. "We love your work." Adam had said to her just two days ago. Adam Quincy Montague was Sarah's supervisor and mentor. "Your name came up at the Partner's meeting. It's going to happen soon, Sarah." The Partner's meeting was two months ago. Adam always said all the right things without really saying the one right thing: "congratulations partner."

The sound of the horn blowing from the car behind Sarah brought her back to the present. Sarah headed home to her small garden condo. The condo sat on a hill overlooking the river. Sarah grabbed the mail, as Tabby, her calico cat, was waiting at the door to greet her, rubbing his face against her leg when she entered. Placing the mail onto the counter, she reached into the cupboard and retrieved the cat treats, holding them in her open hand for Tabby. The red message light on the answering machine was flickering rapidly, indicating that she had received several calls. The first message was from a telemarketer claiming that refinancing rates were at an all-time low. The second message was from her sister asking if she could loan her fifty bucks until payday. The last message was from Thornton. It had been left on the machine only fifteen minutes ago. He wanted to know why she was spying on him, and exactly what she had overheard while standing outside of his office.

At first Sarah was offended by the accusation, then angered. How dare he accuse her of spying? Thornton had been shouting. Anyone within 50 feet of his office would have easily overheard his conversation. Her intent was to make sure that everything was OK, not make herself privy to a private conversation. Besides, what was so important in his conversation that Thornton would call her at home? He had never called her at home before. Sarah tried to recall exactly what she had heard during his phone conversation. It was something to the effect that he had gone too far. The lawyer in Sarah began to work. What could Thornton be involved in that would cause him to go too far? Just how far was too far? Had Thornton done something unethical or, worse, had he committed a crime? The same analytical mind that had brought Sarah to the top of her class was working reflexively now. Whatever it was, Thornton was worried that someone other than the person on the other end of that telephone conversation had found out; worried enough to call her at home.

Sarah decided against calling Thornton back. She wasn't quite sure what she'd say to him anyway. Besides, he didn't know that she was at home or had even heard his message. Just then the phone rang. Sarah stared at the receiver, unsure of whether she was ready to deal with Thornton. Another ring, then another, Sarah breathed deeply, then picked up the phone. "Listen Thornton, I wasn't eavesdropping on you."

"Ms. Davenport?" It was a female's voice on the other end. "Ms. Davenport, I must speak to you. I think that there is something you need to know. Can you come right over?" The request was spoken softly, but with a hint of desperation.

Sarah wanted nothing more than to take a long soak in a hot bubble bath, but recognizing Jill Archer as the caller, she made a valiant effort to keep the reluctance from her voice. "Certainly Mrs. Archer, I'll be right there." After all, clients of the Archers' status didn't come along every day.

Sarah grabbed her coat, purse and car keys before heading out the door. She found herself traveling in the opposite direction from which she had just come. She wondered what could be so important that it couldn't wait until morning. The firm expected their attorneys to put in long hours. Sarah was no exception, often working seventy to eighty hours a week. What was another couple of hours in an already long day? She had been to the Archer's home twice before. Mrs. Archer preferred to meet there. It was easier to maintain privacy. No press could get through the gates without an invitation.

Sarah had just pulled the car out into the street when her cell phone rang. Sarah reached across the seat for her purse and pulled out the phone. Answering the phone, a frantic voice was on the other end. "Please tell me that you're on your way. I can't keep this secret anymore." The pitch of her voice had increased with each word. "Please, hurry!" Sarah heard glass breaking in the background.

Sarah sped up, her left hand firmly clutching the steering wheel, her right hand holding the cell phone to her ear. "Is everything alright Mrs. Archer? Do you need me to call the police?"

"No!" Jill Archer screamed. "I'm OK, I simply dropped a glass. Please don't call the police or anyone else. Right now you're the only one I trust. I know that everything I say to you will be kept confidential. No one else must find out."

"Who the hell are you talking to? Get off the phone!" Someone shouted. It sounded like John Archer. "Give me that damned phone!" Sarah was sure she recognized the distinctive voice that had verbally attacked her this afternoon. Sarah heard Mrs. Archer gasp, and the sound of the phone hitting hard against the floor.

Sarah sat frozen for several seconds. She wasn't aware that she'd been holding her breath until she was forced to inhale. Realizing what had happened, she shouted into the phone: "Mrs. Archer?!? Hello? Hello!" The line was dead.

Sarah knew John Archer had a temper. Would he actually hurt his wife? She wasn't sure. She had no idea what she would do when she arrived at the Archer's house. She was acting more on instinct. She only knew that she had to get there, and get there quickly. Sarah headed out of the city. The Archer's estate was several acres. The road leading up to the house was studded with street lamps on either side. Sarah suddenly took note of what she was doing and an icy fear ran down her spine. Taking several deep breaths she attempted to calm herself. Approaching the house the gates opened. She was obviously expected. She drove up the semi-circular driveway and stopped in front of the house. She had to know what was going on, whether Mrs. Archer was all right. Despite her trepidation she exited her vehicle.

Taking another deep breath Sarah went up to the door and rang the bell. She waited. Nothing. Again she rang the bell. Nothing. Sarah stepped back away from the door and went to a side window and peered in. She could see that the room was in disarray. And wait, was that...she could see a woman's leg. Yes; there was a woman on the floor lying lifelessly. Sarah rushed to the front door and started banging on it, "Hello" Sarah yelled. "Mrs. Archer, Mr. Archer!" Sarah tried the doorknob. It turned. The door was unlocked. Sarah went in. Stepping through the doorway, out of the corner of her eye, she saw a dark figure. A man. He was coming at her fast. He had been waiting for her to open the door. She tried to turn around. It was too late. Sarah felt intense pain on the right side of her skull, but only for a second, she was out cold.

Chapter 2

Back at the office Thornton had received a late visitor. It was Marconi - the person Thornton had been speaking with earlier, and the last person that he wanted to see. Marconi was short and thick, with menacing eyes. Standing with his shoulders juxtaposed against the door frame, he took up most of the available space. His nonverbal communication was clear - you don't go anywhere unless and until I allow you to leave.

"Hello Thornton."

The sound of Marconi's voice raised the hairs on the back of Thornton's neck. He dared not raise his head for fear of losing it. With eyes lowered, darting, Thornton replied nervously: "What are you doing here?"

"I was worried that you may not fully understand our arrangement." Marconi took a couple of steps into the office.

"No, no, I understand perfectly." Thornton said nervously as he sat there trying not to move a muscle, wishing he could disappear.

"Just so we're clear," Marconi sneered. "You need to make sure that all is well."

Thornton was confused and wondered what he had done to elicit this visit. Did Marconi have doubts about him? Had he come to kill him? Thornton anxiously looked around and wondered if the secutiry guard, Chester, would hear his screams. "What do you mean?"

"When we were on the phone earlier, I thought I heard your door slam shut. Was there a problem?" Did I upset you?

"No, not at all. I was just making sure that no one heard our conversation". Marconi also wanted to be sure. He stared straight at Thornton, noting the uneasy twitch of his upper lip, the slight shake of his left hand, and the rapid movement of his eyes. "Who could have possibly overheard our conversation?"

"No one. I mean…" Thornton was not a good liar. "Well, there was another attorney in the office. I saw her shadow in the hallway when we were on the phone, but she didn't hear anything." It sounded as if Thornton was trying to convince himself that this was true.

In a very calm voice, a voice you use when you are in complete control, Marconi replied "Are you sure? You can't afford to be wrong. I can't afford for you to be wrong. For your sake, Thornton, you better make sure."

"Make sure?" Thornton asked.

"Yes, make sure."

Thornton quickly blurted out, "I'll take care of it. Don't worry"

Just as stealthily as he had appeared, Marconi was gone.

****

"Ms. Davenport, are you OK?" Sarah could barely hear the voice. She looked up. The uniform quickly told her that it was a police officer. "Are you OK? Do you need a doctor"?

"No, no I think I'm OK."

"That's a pretty nice-sized bump you have there," The Officer said.

The Officer helped Sarah sit upright.

"What happened," Sarah asked. "Where's Mrs. Archer?"

"I'm sorry, Ms. Davenport, Mrs. Archer is dead."

The words hit Sarah hard. Her first thoughts went to Mr. Archer. That Bastard! How could he? Sarah's head was spinning. As she tried to recall what happened, she realized that it must have been Mrs. Archer lying on the floor. She remembered being struck by a man. He'd come at her so fast that she barely got a glimpse of him. Try as she might, she could not recall one identifying feature. Sarah thought hard, but the Officer interrupted her thoughts.

"Ms. Davenport, can you tell me what you were doing here"?

Sarah gathered her thoughts. She told him about the phone call, her arrival at the

Archer house, and the last thing she saw before being knocked unconscious.

"How did you know my name? Who called the police, and where's Mr. Archer? Sarah asked all at once.

"I found your driver's license in your purse. Someone tripped the silent alarm. We don't know where Mr. Archer is, we're checking on that now. We better get you to a hospital."

"No, no I'm OK."

Just then a squad arrived and two paramedics entered the house. One went over to check on Mrs. Archer. The other proceeded to examine the bump on Sarah's head. The skin was not broken, but the redness and swelling were signs of a possible concussion. The paramedic recommended that she be transported to a hospital. Sarah was still feeling slightly disoriented, and had a throbbing headache, but felt she would be all right with a little rest

The Officer and paramedic helped Sarah up and into one of the dining room chairs.

The paramedic then headed back outside. Sarah massaged her temples in a slow circular motion. Looking around Sarah began to take in her surroundings. There were a half dozen uniformed police officers moving throughout the house. Mrs. Archer lay at the base of the stairwell in the foyer next to an antique mahogany desk. Someone had thrown a sheet over her body. A bright crimson stain soaked the upper left corner of the sheet. Droplets of blood also splattered the iridescent ceramic tile not far from where she lay. Sarah couldn't stand the sight of blood. It had always made her queasy. She had to get out of here.

Just as Sarah decided to leave, the officer who initially stood over her informed her that the homicide detective had arrived and needed to ask her some questions.

"Can't this wait until later? I'll come down to the police station tomorrow and answer all the questions you have. Right now I only want to get out of here."

From behind her Sarah heard a rich baritone voice reply "As much as I'd like to grant your request, I'm afraid that won't be possible. Only in the movies does the beautiful witness get to come to the police station the next day. In the real world the first few hours are crucial to the investigation."

Sarah turned to address the man who had just entered the room. He was extremely tall and good-looking, sexy even. He had dark hair and dark eyes that seemed to penetrate her very soul. Sarah couldn't help but stare as he proceeded across the room to her side. Strangely, she found herself unable to speak. Sarah was surprised by her reaction to this man. She had certainly seen good-looking men before. Yet this man seemed to have an overwhelming effect on her senses. Maybe she was experiencing some bazaar after effect from getting conked on the head.

Finally finding her voice Sarah asked, "Are you the homicide detective?"

"I am Detective Jake Reed, at your service." He had a dazzling smile, which sent goose bumps down her spine. He was arrogantly self-assured, tilting his head in her direction.

Jake extended his right hand, which Sarah was slow to grasp. He had strong lean fingers that were well manicured. His grip was firm, but surprisingly gentle. "Sarah, Sarah Davenport."

"Well Mrs. Davenport…"

"It's Ms." Sarah quickly interjected.

Detective Reed flashed a cocky little grin that would have been irritating on a less confident man. He recognized the opening, and took a quick glance over Sarah, noticing how athletic she was. Jake quickly discarded the thought. This was work, and he needed to be professional.

"Excuse me, I stand corrected . . . Ms. Davenport. I promise not to keep you long, but it is imperative that I get this information as quickly as possible. The paramedic said that you did not want to be taken to the hospital. If that's the case I'd like to ask you a few questions here. Is the chair you're sitting in comfortable?"

"Yes, the chair is fine." Sarah watched as Jake pulled a matching chair from under the table and set it adjacent to hers. She suddenly felt like she could tell this man anything. Something about him inspired trust.

"If you would, start at the beginning and tell me what happened." Jake was all business. Gone was the charming man who had put her at ease with his mild manner and appreciative gaze. In his place was the quintessential detective. His attention was completely focused. His dark eyes did not blink, they simply watched - taking in every expression and each gesture as Sarah recanted tonight's events.

Detective Reed sat quietly, jotting down a few notes, giving Sarah all the time she needed to tell what had happened at her own pace. He hated when a detective would continually interrupt witnesses, making them lose their train of thought. Consequently, pertinent information would be inadvertently left out. Witnesses would believe that they had relayed the whole story when in actuality they had failed to provide minute yet relevant facts.

When Sarah finished her re-enactment, Jake replayed her statement in his head, quickly analyzing the information. He was certain that he could rule Sarah out as a potential suspect. She had no motive that he could detect; she was found injured and unconscious at the scene; and she appeared to be straightforward and honest. Jake was a pro at reading people. He was trained to spot deceptive behavior. This woman was no murderer. The more he thought about her, the more his thoughts turned away from work. She was in fact someone he could see himself dating. She was beautiful; smart; independent; definitely his kind of woman.

Refocusing, Jake asked, "On what grounds did Mrs. Archer file for divorce?"

"Mental cruelty." Sarah replied. "She claimed that her husband was constantly belittling her and the children. She refused to acknowledge whether or not he'd been physically abusive, but I always suspected that he had."

"If you suspected physical violence why didn't you call the police when you received her phone call?"

Although his tone was not accusatory, Sarah thought she detected a hint of condemnation in his eyes. "I wish I would have. Maybe she would still be alive. I didn't stop to think. I just reacted.

"No one's blaming you Ms. Davenport. I think that you are a very courageous woman. By coming here you put your client's welfare ahead of your own safety." He smiled teasingly. "That is something attorneys are not known for doing." He was trying to make her feel better. "Can you tell me what time you received Mrs. Archer's phone call?"

"About 7:15 pm. I spent another late night at the office and didn't arrive home until around seven. She called shortly after I got home."

"How do you know it was Mr. Archer on the other end of the phone, or that he was the person who struck you?"

"When Mrs. Archer called me I heard her husband's voice in the background. His voice was raised in anger just as it had been earlier today when he called my office. I once ran into Mr. Archer when I came to the house to meet with Mrs. Archer. He is of similar size and weight as the man who came at me from the shadows."

"Did you believe that Mr. Archer would carry out the threats he made against you and his wife?

"No, I mean yes, I knew that he would put up a good fight in the courtroom. I've dealt with bullies of his sort before, but I never believed that he'd actually commit murder.

"You've had quite a day Ms. Davenport. I think that any remaining questions can wait until tomorrow. Would you like me to have an officer drive you home?"

"No, I'm feeling much better now. My car's right out front."

Sarah stood to take her leave and was overcome with dizziness. She blindly reached out to grab hold of the chair but found Jakes arm instead. With lightning fast reflexes, Jake reached out to support Sarah before she could fall. He grabbed her by the waist and slowly pulled her to her feet. Sarah leaned into his body, which was as solid as a support beam. The scent of his cologne wafted lightly into her nostrils, causing an intoxicating allure, so much so that the moment seemed surreal.

Sparks flew. Sarah was overcome with need. Never before had she experienced such a strong physical attraction. Sarah looked up into Jakes eyes for any sign that he too felt the connection between them. His face was unreadable. Disappointed, she dropped her gaze. Jake called out to a uniformed officer with instructions that he and his partner drive Sarah and her car home. Sarah tried to protest, but was too exhausted to put up much of a fight.

Jake escorted Sarah out and placed her in the passenger side of her car. Officer Ceckitti would drive her home while Officer Shaw followed behind in a cruiser. Jake reached across Sarah's lap as he pulled the seat belt across her body and snapped it into place. Jake smiled at her. "It's the law you know."

He provided her with a business card. "If you remember anything else, call me right away, no matter what time of day." He turned to say something to Officer Ceckitti, and then told her he'd be in touch, then gently shut her door. Sarah couldn't help but notice that even in the way he shut the door, Jake was firm, yet gentle. This was ridiculous. Sarah laid her head back and closed her eyes. When the police cruiser reached the end of the driveway they were bombarded by the media. Reporters were swarming along the outer perimeter of the property. They began shouting questions at her and the officers, seeking information about the murder. Sarah opened and then closed her eyes tightly. This made her head hurt worse than before. She wished this were all a dream. Officer Ceckitti rolled up his window and proceeded on, ignoring the reporter's requests.

****

Jake knew that the media was out there waiting at the end of the driveway, scrambling to get a story. He'd give them a statement later, after he obtained more facts and had a clearer picture of what took place. He was pleased that the initial responding officers had secured the scene so quickly. The media would often trample through a crime scene corrupting the evidence. As he entered the house he reviewed the crime log and the statement written by the first officer at the scene. There appeared to be no witnesses other than Sarah and the murderer.

The coroner would pinpoint the time of death and the potential cause. Forensic evidence was being bagged and tagged by the Crime Scene Unit. The house and grounds were being thoroughly searched, photographed, and dusted for prints. He would personally do the blood splatter analysis. The crime lab was tremendously backlogged due to a shortage of trained technicians. Lab results were generally not being processed for several weeks. He would have to charm Judy, the typist clerk at the lab, to get her to put his request at the top of the stack. He had just given the order to transport Mrs. Archer's body to the coroner's office when he heard a commotion outside the front door. It was Mr. Archer demanding entry into his house.

****

Jake's first impression upon seeing Archer was that he was a force to be reckoned with. He was an extremely large man, as tall as Jake, but more broad at the shoulders. He had a barreled chest that looked massive despite, or maybe because of, his tailored Armani suit. Other than his wedding ring he was unadorned by jewelry or accessories of any kind. Definitely a no frills type of guy. He appeared to be a man accustomed to giving orders and having them obeyed.

As Jake approached, Archer demanded to know what was going on. "Where's my wife?!?" Jake introduced himself and offered his sympathy as he explained to him that his wife was dead. Mr. Archer appeared to be stunned.

"Dead. Where is she? I demand to see her now!" Archer exclaimed, as he rushed towards the house.

Jake grabbed hold of his arm. "Mr. Archer, I can't allow you to enter the house at this time."

"Get your goddamned hand off of me. Do you have any idea whom you're dealing with?" His nostrils flared as he fought to control his rising temper. "This is my wife that we are talking about. You have no right to keep me away from her."

"Mr. Archer, as I explained to you, your wife is dead, and her death appears to be a homicide. As the lead detective I have every right to conduct my investigation in whatever way I deem necessary." Jake had dealt with bereaved family members in the past. Sometimes they expressed their grief in the form of anger as Mr. Archer was now doing. However, John Archer's brand of arrogance and condescension rubbed Jake the wrong way.

Archer barely contained his anger. "Son, I'm the wrong guy to piss off. Not only am I a personal friend of your police chief, but I know the mayor as well. If you're not careful you could end up pounding the beat during the graveyard shift along with the rookies."

"Officer Wright," Jake called out and turned to the uniformed officer standing beside him. "Please place Mr. Archer in the back of the cruiser".

"Are you arresting me?" Archer asked

"No, you're simply being detained for questioning".

"I'm calling my lawyer, now!" Archer exclaimed as he reached for his cell phone. The officer grabbed Archer's arm just above the elbow and was thrown off balance as Archer pulled away. "I run a multimillion dollar corporation. I think that I can successfully walk myself to the car." Archer headed towards the nearest cruiser. Once inside, Archer promptly phoned his attorney who told him to remain quiet until he arrived. Archer was white-hot mad.

Mrs. Archer's body was carried out of the house on a stretcher. Mr. Archer was let out of the cruiser so that he could view the body before it was transported to the morgue. Jake watched Archer carefully as the sheet was removed from his wife's body. Archer's face remained expressionless. There was no viable hint of emotion. Was Archer always this cold? Did he not give a damn that his wife was dead, or was he one of those men who kept his feelings close to the vest? As the squad drove away with the body, Archer was escorted back to the cruiser.

Jake was giving final instructions to the officers who would remain at the scene when Archer's attorney arrived. Archer must be paying his attorney one heck of a retainer fee to warrant such a quick response. The attorney, Nathan Sims, a well known corporate lawyer, approached Jake and wanted to know why his client was being detained. Jake explained the circumstance to Sims and advised him that Archer was simply being held for questioning.

Sims advised Jake that he was not going to allow Archer to answer any questions until he had been given an opportunity to consult with his client. Jake explained that Archer was a suspect in his wife's murder and would remain so until the evidence proved otherwise. He told Sims that the best way to eliminate Archer as a suspect was for him to advise his client to cooperate with the investigation. The police could then pursue other leads and other possible suspects. Archer was let out of the cruiser and allowed to privately discuss the matter with his attorney. Shortly thereafter they agreed to cooperate and meet Jake at the police station for questioning. They all left the crime scene and headed into the station.

When Archer and his attorney arrived in the interrogation room Jake immediately started asking questions.

"Did you love your wife Mr. Archer?"

"Of course I did." Archer clenched his teeth as he glared at Jake.

"Mr. Archer can you explain your whereabouts between the hours of 7:00 pm and 8:00 pm this evening." Jake said, totally unfazed by Archer's visible hostility.

"You don't have to answer that." Sims advised.

"I don't mind answering the detective's questions, I have nothing to hide". Archer said. "I can tell you exactly where I was during that time period. I was meeting with my wife's divorce attorney. Sarah Davenport."

His reply threw Jake for a loop. How was that possible Jake thought? Evidently Mr. Archer was unaware that Sarah was at his house during that hour or had been found lying unconscious next to his wife's body. Maybe Archer was not the killer after all. There was no way that he would attempt to use Sarah as an alibi if he knew she had been found lying unconscious not far from his dead wife. "Where did you meet Ms. Davenport?" Jake asked.

"Well I didn't actually meet with her, but I attempted to do so. I went to her office to drop off some financial records that she had requested, only to find out that she had already left for the day."

"So there's no way to prove that you were where you say you were".

"Well if my word is not good enough, and it appears that it's not, then I suggest that you check with the building security guard. I told him that I was there to see Ms. Davenport and he said that she had already left for the evening. I explained that I had an important financial document for her. He told me where her office was. In fact, I had to sign into a log book before he'd let me up. When I realized that she had gone I turned and left.

"What time were you there." Jake asked.

"I arrived at her office around 7:30 in the evening and was there for about ten minutes."

Jake knew that it was at least a half an hour drive from the Archer's estate to the downtown area where the law firm was located. If Ms. Archer had been alive at 7:15pm as Sarah claimed, and Mr. Archer was telling the truth about his whereabouts, then he could not have killed his wife. Jake would need to get a hold of the phone records first thing in the morning, and confirm Archer's alibi with the security guard. For now it seemed that he would have to let Archer go. "Mr. Archer, where are your children?"

"The boys are away at private school. I intend to send for them right away."

"It's just as well that the kids are away. Until police investigators are finished processing the scene, no one is to enter the house. Just one last question, "do you know of anyone who would want to kill your wife?"

"No. I can't think of anyone except... her drug dealer."

Chapter 3

By the time Sarah arrived home it was late and she was exhausted. She made her way into the condo with the assistance of Officer Ceckitti, and prepared an ice pack for her mildly throbbing head. Unbeknownst to Sarah, outside and across the street, sitting quietly in his leased blue sedan, sat Thornton. When he saw Sarah exit the patrol car with a police escort, he was startled. There was another Officer driving Sarah's car. Thornton decided it was best to get out of there. He started the engine and eased the car into the street. He'd have to wait for another opportunity to confront Sarah.

****

The next morning was beautiful. The sun beamed in through Sarah's bedroom window, warming her face and causing her to awaken. She opened her eyes and immediately squinted from the bright rays of sunshine. She started to sit up, and was quickly reminded of her bruise. The pain, though not so unbearable, was definitely noticeable. It was a stark reminder that Mrs. Archer was dead. Sarah glanced over at the clock and realized that she had overslept. She hadn't remembered to set the alarm the night before. Sarah picked up the phone and called the Office.

Adam was understanding, and seemed genuinely concerned. He knew Mrs. Archer was Sarah's client and had seen Sarah's picture on the news. Sarah assured him that she would be fine, but he wanted her to take a few days off and rest anyway.

As Sarah hung up the phone she wondered about Thornton. She still was not ready to address Thornton's absurd accusation. She lay back down and dozed off. She awakened around ten. This time she forced herself out of bed and into the kitchen. Coffee. Sarah needed a good strong cup of Joe to settle her thoughts and help her focus . . . Detective Jake Reed. Sarah smiled as she recalled meeting the tall, dark, extremely sexy detective. She thought about calling him. She wished he were there now.

It had been over a year since Sarah had broken things off with Derek. What a jerk he turned out to be. Sarah had never been the type of person to subordinate herself to anyone. Always independent, always a fierce competitor, Sarah knew what she wanted and knew how to go about getting it. She was not ready for a family, and she certainly was not ready to settle down and become a housewife. A housewife! Why even if she were ready to have a baby, she would never be able to stay at home for the rest of her life. She needed her own life. She needed to be independent. Sure, she'd love to have children someday, but never with a man who wanted her to forsake who she was for who he wanted her to be. No, the type of man Sarah needed was the type of man who understood her, a man who recognized her independent spirit, but at the same time recognized that her independence did not jeopardize his manliness. She needed someone who was strong, but also gentle, a self-assured man, a man like Jake Reed.

The coffee was good, and just what the doctor ordered.

****

Thornton was in his office on the phone. He was explaining that he was not sure how much Sarah had heard, but she wasn't in yet; probably avoiding him. He was saying that he would get to the bottom of things right away. He explained that he waited for her to come home last night, but when she finally arrived, she had a police escort.

"Are you kidding?" Thornton said. "I was getting the heck out of there." He paused and listened. "Well, she didn't show up today. I'm going to pay her a visit as soon as I can get away from here." Another pause. "Yes Sir. I know. I'll take care of it."

Thornton hung up the telephone. He had no idea how he was going to "take care of it." He certainly was not up to any violence. He had never so much as had a verbal argument, let alone become involved in any type of physical altercation. Thornton thought back to the sixth grade, when Bradley and Shawn used to bully him at every opportunity. They would knock his books out of his hand for no reason other than to humiliate him. How Thornton wished he could fight. He would sit in class and daydream about punching the daylights out of both of them. A smile would curl its way onto Thornton's face. Oh the tremendous sense of satisfaction he would derive as he pounded them into the ground. All of his classmates would know that Thornton Hilliard was someone to be reckoned with. The girls would think him a hero. He would be popular and he would have friends. All of a sudden the bell would ring, and he would shake with fear knowing what was to come.

Thornton hated violence, most probably because he was always on the receiving end. But this time he had to do something. He could never go to jail. The thought of what would happen to a man like him in a place like that was enough to make him say that he'd

"take care of it." He was in way over his head.
He should have never gotten involved.

Thornton processed patent applications.
Patents made perfect sense for Thornton. It
was a safe and, except for the occasional
disagreement with the Patent and Trademark
Office, mostly non-confrontational area of law
within which to practice. Thornton processed
patent applications and oversaw patents for
several large companies, including Jackrabbit,
Inc. Jackrabbit specialized in stem- cell
research and production. Just last week,
Jackrabbit became the first and only company
in the world to actually grow a human heart in
the laboratory using stem cells.

It was really quite simple in its
brilliance. Jackrabbit first took a few heart cells
from the diseased heart of a patient, and
extracted the genome. It then copied the
genome into stem- cells that the company grew
from previously harvested developing
embryos. As the cells multiplied, they took on
the form and function of the heart cells; they
actually started pulsating rhythmically, like a
little tiny heart, but without the form. The
heart cells were constantly examined, and any
sign of disease was removed. The healthiest
cells were allowed to multiply, and in a few
weeks, the pulsating mass would take shape,
and a new heart was beginning. Best of all,
because the heart was grown using, in part, a

patient's own cells, the body would accept the new heart as its own. The heart was the first, and possibly the most important of human organs, and Jackrabbit had concentrated its early efforts on the heart, but Jackrabbit was in the process of expanding its methods to other human organs.

Imagine the possibilities. People could replace worn organs as easily as they replaced worn car parts. Restoring a person to mint condition was now as much a reality as refurbishing that old jalopy in the garage. People could theoretically live forever. There were billions to be made - billions one could only imagine. Marconi apparently knew it. Marconi also knew of Thornton's other dark secret - his penchant for gambling and, the not so occasional professional female companion.

Thornton was not a very good gambler, but he loved what gambling could provide. Gambling, more than anything else, made Thornton believe that he was somebody. Thornton felt power when he was at the craps tables; money, drinks, and women were all a fingertip away. It didn't matter so much that he lost, because Marconi was always willing to extend another line of credit. "Don't worry Thornton; you'll pay me back someday. Don't forget, I know where you work. Ha ha ha, ha ha ha ha." Thornton would return the laugh with a nervous little chuckle of his own. The momentary discomfort was quickly replaced with the feeling of cash in his hands - a now familiar feeling. Here he was again, the high roller, back at the tables, the drinks, and the women at his disposal.

Thornton was not an attractive man, but Thornton was smart. He had a doctoral degree in molecular biology and a law degree. He spent all of his twenties in school. There weren't many dates, and it was during this time that Thornton had discovered the wonderful world of prostitution. All one needed was cash. With the right amount of money, Thornton was made to feel as if he was one of the most powerful and handsome men on the planet. It was those moments that Thornton carried with him. He didn't think about how cold and callous the women could be once the money ran out. He dwelled on the positive. It was the same with the "line of credit" that Marconi was so willing to extend to Thornton. Thornton thought about what he could do with the money, not about how or when he would have to pay it back.

Marconi knew, seemed to have known all along that Thornton would someday be able to repay him - in spades. And when Marconi and two of his seasoned minions finally approached Thornton about repaying the debt, a debt that had ballooned to over $400,000 over the past 18 months, Thornton quickly caved.

Thornton was scrambling around for something to throw at Marconi to assure him that he could cover the debt when Marconi uttered the word Jackrabbit. Thornton was caught off guard. Marconi, knowing he had caught Thornton off guard, said the name again; Jackrabbit. I want the Jackrabbit patent. Now!

Thornton knew he was in trouble. But left with the choice of imminent physical harm or the possibility of prison at some point in the future, he quickly retrieved the patent application file. "I'll need to make a copy."

"Hurry." Said Marconi. Upon returning, after having a moment to think about what he was doing, Thornton tried to explain to Marconi that he would find a way to eventually repay him. He would take out a loan, or sell his condo. Marconi, however, was only interested in the patent application. Thornton handed over the papers, and Marconi left.

Sitting at his desk now, having recently violated the United States Code, for which he could spend a considerable amount of time in a Federal Institution, Thornton ruminated over the mounting problems he faced. He also had Sarah to worry about. How was he going to "take care of it." Where was Sarah? He could hardly be expected to show up at her house in the middle of the day. He should have never called her and left that message. But he had no choice. Marconi had paid Thornton a visit at the office that night. He wanted to be extra sure that Thornton wouldn't do anything to jeopardize their partnership. If only Thornton was a better liar. Why couldn't he keep a straight face and tell Marconi that there was nothing to worry about? Because he wasn't a good liar. Instead, Marconi paid Thornton a visit, and the visit had frightened Thornton enough to make him call Sarah at home.

Maybe Thornton has scared Sarah with his call? The thought amused him. He had never scared anyone in his life. Yeah, maybe Sarah was afraid of him. The more he thought about it, the more the idea appealed to him. He started to believe that it might just be possible. Why else had she not returned his call? And why hadn't she come to work today? She was afraid of him! But what about her police escort last night? Where had she been? Maybe that had something to do with her not showing up for work today. Maybe SHE was in trouble. If she was, maybe he could find out what it was that she was involved in and use that to blackmail her. She would certainly keep her mouth shut if that were the case. But how could he find out? It wasn't as if he knew anyone at the police station.

Someday he would be so powerful that he would have police contacts at his disposal. With one phone call he'd be able to get all the information on anyone that he wanted. For now, Thornton would have to confront Sarah. Was she afraid of him or not? Was he afraid of her? Two things were certain: he was afraid of Marconi, and he was afraid of going to prison. He had to confront her. Thornton grabbed his coat and headed out the door.

****

Sarah had just finished a long, hot shower. Sometimes, nothing felt so good. She dressed and sat down to read the morning paper. The front-page headline was a story about the administration justifying, for a different reason this time, taking the Nation to war. Sarah flipped over to the metro section to see whether the story about Jill Archer had made the morning paper. There it was. There was a picture of Mrs. Archer and beneath it the story of how she was found dead in her home. Mysteriously there was no mention of Mr. Archer. A knock at the door interrupted Sarah's reading. Sarah peered through the peephole and there stood Thornton. "Who is it?" Sarah said, more out of habit than anything else.

"It's Thornton. You weren't at the office today, and I was wondering if you were alright"? They both knew that this was a lie, and as soon as Thornton said it he wished he could take it back. Sarah played along. "I'm OK." Thornton was no good at this. Now he was stuck, with the message that he had left on the answering machine hanging in the air like thick smoke. "Sarah, I . . . " then he remembered the police escorting Sarah home last night, and he decided to lie again. "The police came by the office this morning looking for you." He let it hang in the air, hoping she would bite.

Sarah gave it some consideration. She tried to recall the last words she and Jake Reed had spoken. He said that they would talk tomorrow, which was today, so it was possible that he could have stopped by the office to speak with her. In fact she had hoped that she would see Jake today. For a moment Sarah forgot about the message that Thornton had left on her answering machine. She opened the door and asked, "Did he leave his name, the officer who stopped by the office?"

Thornton was so overcome by his successful lie that he forgot for a moment what he was doing. "No, neither one of them, they were just a couple of uniformed officers. I don't know what they wanted, but they had asked for you." Thornton was thinking now, remembering why he was there. He had to know what she knew. How much of his conversation with Marconi had she overheard?

"You're sure they had on uniforms?" Sarah asked.

"Of course I'm sure. It's kind of hard to miss those ugly five-point hats they wore, or their shiny guns and badges. Why all the interest? I thought it was no big deal. They came in and asked for you, then left."

Sarah wondered if the officers would be coming here next. Maybe Jake wanted to see her and had sent uniformed officers to pick her up. Thornton had moved inside the door now. He started thinking that maybe he could bluff his way through this encounter. He remembered last night, and said "I heard them say something about last night." Again he left the bait hanging in the air. "Sarah, are you in some kind of trouble?"

"No, it's nothing like that. Last night I went to check on a client, and when I arrived at her house, she was dead."

"What!" Thornton exclaimed with a hint of fear and excitement. "I can't imagine finding a dead body. Who was she?"

Sarah's mouth was suddenly dry and her eyes began to tear up as she recalled the previous night events. Her voice was barely audible, but Thornton was watching her lips move as she replied, "Jill Archer. Wife of John Archer."

"THE John Archer?"

"That's the one." Sarah said with a quick nod to her head.

Thornton had heard of John Archer, the multi-millionaire, whose savvy investments were legendary. This was interesting news, fascinating even. A client at his firm had been murdered, a client with a rich and powerful husband. This was definitely news. He should have taken time to read the paper this morning, but he'd been too caught up in his own thoughts. Surely the news article provided the name of the law firm. They may have even mentioned some of the more prominent attorneys' names. Thornton's name had been printed in the paper once before. After a client who passed away had his patent rights tied up in a very public probate dispute. Thornton cleaned out the newspaper stand that day. He clipped the article out, highlighted his name and framed two copies. One was now hanging in his office, the other in the living room of his home. Thornton's smile began to recede as he remembered again why he had come. He decided to broach the subject. "About yesterday. . ."

Sarah cut him off. "Look Thornton, I don't know what you've gotten yourself into." Thornton froze. Sarah started to continue, but she noticed the change in Thornton's expression and body language. She remembered the message, and what she had overheard: that he had gone too far as it was. Thinking that the police might be on their way, she said, "Whatever it is, maybe the police can help?"

"No!" Thornton composed himself. "No. The police must be kept out of it." Thornton realized that he had exposed his fear. His eyes narrowed. His head began to pound. He had come here to confront her, and here he was. Now was the time. Were it not for her eavesdropping, none of this would be necessary. He hated her at this moment. She had created a situation that he had no idea how to handle. He was frustrated and afraid.

Sarah's curiosity was piqued. She knew something was bothering Thornton a great deal, it was written all over his face, and whatever it was, he was afraid of the police finding out. She decided to throw out some bait of her own. "Thornton, you're in a lot of trouble." She watched as the color drained from Thornton's face. He started to tremble. "Maybe I can help." Sarah said with sincerity.

Thornton looked at Sarah imploringly. "I should have never gotten involved. They forced me to tell them Sarah, don't you see I had no choice."

"What I see is a good man with a problem that is escalating out of control." Sarah placed her hand lightly on Thornton's forearm. Her manner was calm and reassuring. "If we go to the police I'm sure that they could help. Tell them your side of the story, whatever it is."

Thornton looked up, and was face to face with Sarah. Their eyes met, and he could tell that she was sincere, and for the first time he realized that maybe Sarah could be of some help. He also noticed, if only briefly, how beautiful Sarah was. But the police were not an option. The thought of having to face Marconi and his two goons was implausible. "Sarah, there's simply no way we can go to the police. I know I shouldn't have told him about Jackrabbit, but I had no choice. He was threatening to hurt me. And if I go to the police, there's no telling what they'll do to me."

"Jackrabbit?"

"Yes. The pending patent."

So that was it. Sarah didn't know much about patents, but she did know that they were big business. The Intellectual Property Division was a huge moneymaker for the firm. She also knew that the information was confidential. Disclosing information about a pending new drug or computer chip could be worth millions, if not billions of dollars. But whom had he told? Who was on the other end of the phone that night?

****

Jake rolled out of bed shortly before dawn. He had always been an early riser, never requiring more than five or six hours of sleep per night. This often worked to his advantage, and it did today. This latest murder investigation would require a lot of legwork. This was probably the most high profile case that he'd ever been assigned. He'd been on the force for sixteen years. For the first five years he worked an inner city patrol beat on the west side. He was known as the hotshot rookie who had rescued five hostages during a bank robbery. He loved his job. Every day was a challenge, a new adventure. Back then he actually believed that good always prevailed over evil. Now he'd seen too many homicides, too many senseless deaths. Many of which remained unsolved.

Jake downloaded several articles about John Archer from the net. It was amazing how much information he could gather from the privacy of his apartment. He often used the Internet to assist him in his investigations. People thought that they lived in their own private worlds, but in reality none of us were immune from the public eye.

Next Jake telephoned the Office. He would send a detective who worked the day shift over to Sarah's office to check out Archer's alibi. Detective Clark was waiting at the door when Chester arrived at the law firm to begin his shift. Detective Clark introduced himself to Chester, and explained that he needed to see last night's log. Chester showed the log to Detective Clark, and there, with an entry of 7:32 p.m. was John Archer. Detective Clark asked Chester if he remembered seeing Mr. Archer. Chester said sure. Archer dropped off some stuff for Ms. Davenport. He couldn't have stayed more than five or ten minutes. Detective Clark had Chester sign an affidavit attesting to this fact, which he'd left on Jake's desk. It looked as though Archer was in the clear after all.

Jill Archer's doctor was next on Jake's list. John Archer had supplied his name the night before. He explained that his wife had been injured in a car crash nine months ago and had been prescribed highly addictive pain medication. Jake knew that the doctor would claim doctor-patient confidentiality, so he'd procured a court order authorizing the release of Mrs. Archer's medical files. Apparently Jill's doctor had initially prescribed medication to help alleviate the pain in her back caused by a lower disc problem. The doctor claimed to have authorized only three refills, enough for a two-month supply. When Mrs. Archer requested that she be given more pills, he advised her that he was not able to do so because of their addictive potential. Shortly thereafter she discontinued her treatment with him. According to Mr. Archer his wife found a new supplier.

Jake knew people who could assist him in obtaining information on the purchase of illegal drugs. It was not his area of expertise, but his old street partner was now a sergeant in the Narcotics Bureau. He'd contact Eric and see if any of his informants could steer him in the direction of Mrs. Archer's drug supplier. Mr. Archer said that his wife had withdrawn large sums of money in order to pay her dealer. When he became aware of this, he closed her accounts and cut off her cash supply. Could Jill Archer's death have occurred because she owed money to a dealer? Jake didn't know, he only knew that it was his job to find out.

Jake had many more stops to make before the day was through. He wanted one of those stops to be at Sarah Davenport's. He thought of her last night. There were definite possibilities there. He knew that she was attracted to him. He just wasn't sure if he was ready for a new relationship. It had been three months since his last girlfriend, Melanie, moved out, and he was enjoying his freedom. She wanted him to propose, and thought that if she left he'd come running after her. Talk about fantasy worlds, there was no way he was going to propose to her, not today or any day in the foreseeable future. Why is it that women always want to pressure a guy into a commitment? If it's not there, let it go. Move on. Jake was of the school of thought that things worked best when they happened naturally, unforced.

****

"Now that I've told you Sarah, I feel as if a huge weight has been removed."

Sarah was having none of it. Just last night she had attempted to handle a situation that was best left to the professionals. She was not going to make that same mistake again. "By telling me what, that you were forced to tell someone about a patent? I don't know who it is; I don't know anything about patents, and right now I don't want to know. As things stand, I have an ethical duty to report you to the state bar, but Thornton, if you don't go to the police I will." Sarah looked him straight in the eyes with such determination that Thornton knew there was no way of stopping her. His mind started clicking. If he couldn't stop her, maybe he could slow her down.

"Of course you're right. The best chance I have of getting out of this mess is to go to the police. I see that now, and I'm willing to do so, but I need to take care of a personal matter first. I need to go visit my mother at the nursing home. She's been sick for some time now and relies on me for support. It would kill her to hear about this on the news or from someone else. Please Sarah, give me tonight to take care of this. I'll go see the police first thing in the morning. I need your word that you won't share what I told you with another soul until tomorrow."

The silence hung between them as Sarah contemplated Thornton's request. She had a lot of faith in people, but she was no fool. Thornton seemed to be stalling and had agreed to go to the police just a little too quickly, but if his mother really was sick… Thornton could see the branch that Sarah hung from starting to bend. "I know that I don't have the right to ask, but do you think you could possibly come to the police station with me. I could really use the support." Thornton meekly lowered his head.

"OK, I guess there's no harm in waiting until tomorrow." Sarah thought she noted a gleam in Thornton's eyes, and for a brief second she was apprehensive. She quickly dismissed it. Maybe she was being paranoid. They agreed that he would pick her up first thing tomorrow morning.

Chapter 4

As he pulled his car away from the curb, Thornton used his cell phone to call Marconi. There was no way in hell he was going to voluntarily go to the police. The little scene he'd just acted out for Sarah's benefit would buy him some time, but he had to act quickly. Marconi was the surest and best way to handle this new dilemma. He knew that Marconi would put the fear of God in her, just as he had with him. Once she saw how dangerous Marconi was, she'd realize that it was in her best interest to keep her mouth shut.

Marconi had instructed him to drive to the club, which was fine with him because Thornton needed the kind of fix that only a good lap dance would cure. God he hoped it wasn't Candy's day off. She was by far the hottest girl in the place. No one shot his rocket off the way Candy did. When he entered the club she was leaning over a table in the corner serving drinks to two guys who were ogling her overexposed bosom.

Thornton patiently waited. As a boy his mother repeatedly told him that good things were worth the wait. He doubted, however, that she could have imagined anyone like Candy. Her high cut shorts and red halter-top was enough to give him a cavity. Thornton reached into his wallet for a hundred and waived it in her face and she finally walked his way. "Have you got time for me? I've missed you?" he said, patting her rear end.

Candy smiled, snatching the money from Thornton's grasp with such efficiency that even a magician would envy her disappearing skills. "Sure honey, I've always got time for my sugar daddy." Candy pursed her red lips, and then slowly ran her tongue over her upper lip before gently pushing Thornton down in a chair.

Thornton was quickly transported to a fantasy world, where he was floating high above the clouds, then soaring over the mountains, and finally shooting towards the stars. Candy had an amazing body and she knew how to work it. He was about to stick his face in her unbelievable cleavage when she was suddenly and quite unexpectedly plucked from his lap. Thornton quickly looked up to see what had happened and suddenly lost his breath. There stood Marconi, towering and dangerous, power emanating from his pores. Thornton was so wrapped up with Candy that he had completely forgotten about their meeting.

"I know that you did not call me away from important business to bare witness to your perverse pleasures." Marconi's voice was chilling as he looked down at Thornton, who stared silently up at him. "Pull yourself together and meet me at the back booth." Marconi reminded Thornton of a caged bull as he muscled his way past the scattered tables.

Thornton reluctantly rose. Reaching the back booth he took the seat across from Marconi and tried to recall why he was there. Sarah. He had to do something about Sarah and her insistence that he go to the police. Thornton told Marconi that Sara had found out about the pending patent. When asked how she discovered this information Thornton began to sweat. Droplets of perspiration formed on his forehead. Marconi would be furious if he learned that Thornton had told her during a moment of weakness. So he lied and claimed that Sarah had overhead his conversation that night at the office and somehow put the pieces together. He also explained how the police had questioned Sarah after she discovered her client's body. She'd made it clear that he should go to the police in the morning or she'd do it for him.

Marconi sat motionless as he tossed the problem around in his head. He remained calm. Deadly calm. Then slowly rose. "Go home. I'll take care of it", Marconi said in a definitive voice, before exiting the booth and the club.

Thornton should have felt delighted. This was what he wanted. For once he had actually orchestrated a solution. Only Thornton wasn't sure what he had just put into motion. He was relieved that the attention was temporarily diverted away from him. However, he didn't want Sarah hurt, or even worse killed. He couldn't live with that. Maybe he should call and warn her. All she had to do was promise to keep her mouth shut and everything would be fine.

****

Jake had finally arrived at the stop he had most looked forward to today, Sarah Davenport's. What kind of woman was she? She sure made a strong first impression. When it came to people Jake tended to trust his instincts. Sarah said that it was Archer who murdered his wife and assaulted her at his home. Archer, however, had a credible alibi. Jake knew how unreliable an eyewitness could be. At the academy on the first day of training one of the instructors would run through the classroom with a gun and fire several shots. The recruits were then required to give a description. What did the gunman look like, the type and color clothing worn, and the number of shots fired from the weapon? No one ever got it right the first time. Not even Jake. It took training to be able to recall such details at a glance.

Sarah said herself that she did not get a good look at her assailant. All she basically noted was the man's size, hardly a distinguishing identifier. Still, there was something about Sarah that was credible. Maybe he wanted to believe her version of events because he disliked Archer so much. No, Jake would never let his feelings about someone interfere with solving a case. He would follow where the facts led, even if that was somewhere other than Archer. He definitely needed to question Sarah again.

When she answered her door all thoughts of questioning went out the window. How could she possibly look so sexy in a pair of worn jeans and an oversized t-shirt? She had an athletic physique, the kind that would look appealing regardless of how it was clothed. With supreme effort Jake shifted his thoughts from un-wrapping her package to the questioning at hand.

She smiled at him as if she'd been waiting to see him all day and offered him a cup of coffee. He accepted, and casually took note of his surroundings as she went to pour the cup. A slight rubbing along the side of his pant leg alerted him to the fact that he was not alone. Jake looked down to discover a tiger colored cat at his feet, clearly marking its territory.

"Well, I see you've met Tabby. I hope that you're not afraid of cats," Sarah said as she placed the coffee mug on the end table behind him.

"Only the really frisky ones," Jake said, flashing his lopsided grin. "With them you have to expect the unexpected, and even then they find ways to surprise you." Jake made himself comfortable on the tan leather sofa while he took another quick peek at Sarah's shapely curves as she seated herself in a matching chair directly across from him. Jake thought it prudent to get right down to business. "Have you recalled any more details about last night?" Sarah began chewing on her lower lip as she shook her head from side to side. "Do you still believe that it was Archer who hit you over the head?"

"At the time I thought that it was him. Maybe I just expected it to be him. I don't really know anymore." Sarah was frustrated because her memories were unclear. It was getting harder to separate what had actually occurred from what she imagined had occurred. The only thing that seemed real to her right now was Jake Reed. He looked and smelled even better then she remembered.

Jake withdrew a legal size envelope from the black briefcase he had placed beside him on the sofa. As he handed it to Sarah she was surprised to find it contained a list of assets clearly belonging to the Archers. "Were did you get these? Sarah could not imagine what Jake was doing with these documents.

"I had an officer retrieve them from your office this morning. According to John Archer he dropped the papers off to you last night per your request." Jake continued, "I obtained a search warrant to seize the packet that Archer delivered to your office last night. I need you to verify that it was not in your office prior to last evening."

"No it wasn't. A couple of days ago I sent an email to Archer's attorney requesting full financial disclosure, but I never expected Archer to drop it off himself. He had to have done so after I had already left for the day."

"The building security guard, Chester Johnson, placed him in at your office around 7:30 pm. This means he could not have been home at the time of the murder."

Sarah digested the significance of this information. She looked up at Jake. He was staring at her. His intensity was overwhelming as he stared at her. Oh my God. She had accused an innocent man. She would never have knowingly done so. "I have obviously made a mistake, my apologies detective. I can assure you that my intent was not to lead you down a wrong path or point the finger at an innocent person." Sarah was visibly upset.

Jake was immediately contrite. It was not his intent to make her feel bad. "You reported the facts as you saw them Ms. Kelly. No one expects you to do anything less. Jake removed the coffee mug from Sarah's hand. You are still the only significant witness I have in this case. Everything you recall is relevant." Jake took hold of her small delicate hands and clasped them between his own. "At least we know that the man who attacked you was about Archer's size and weight. We know that he was possibly the same man arguing with Ms. Archer before her death and that she was afraid of something or someone. You have gone above and beyond to assist in this case. You have been great. As a matter of fact you have been so great that I was hoping you would consider having dinner with me some evening."

Sarah could not retain the smile that suddenly billowed across her face. Her heart flip-flopped so many times that she thought it was performing an acrobatic show. "Yes, I'll have dinner with you. I thought you'd never ask." As Sarah looked at Jake's expectant face she realized that she had not spoken out loud. "Dinner would be nice," she finally said to Jake.

"Terrific", Jake said, rising to take his leave, pulling Sarah to her feet as well. "I know a wonderful seafood place down by…"

Just then a bullet came whizzing through the living room window shattering the tempered glass.

Jake threw Sarah to the floor, covering her body with his own. He quickly reached into his waistband to retrieve his gun. "Don't move. Stay down on the floor until I get back". Jake kept low to the ground, rapidly making his way out the front door. Arms extended, gun held tightly in his hands, he entered the street taking cover as he swiftly moved along. He did a thorough search of the outer perimeter of the building. He located the shell cases from the bullets that came through Sarah's window, three shots in all. Whoever it was used a silencer. There was no sound to alert the neighbors that shots had been fired. The average citizen would have thought that there were rocks thrown through the window. He knew differently. He'd known immediately that bullets had created the shatter. Were those bullets meant for Sarah or him?

Re-entering Sarah's condo, he called out for her to get up, that the coast was clear. Jake looked for Sarah and realized that she was no longer on the living room floor. Just like a woman to disregard your instructions. She was probably getting something to clean up the glass. Sarah's place was very neat and orderly. She was obviously one of those people who could not abide clutter; everything had to be in its place. Jake began to notice the silence. He went from room to room calling out to Sarah. Nothing. He spotted Tabby curled up on a rug in the corner. There was no sign of Sarah. She was gone.

Chapter 5

Archer was watching intently as Dr. Cho, his lead scientist, read over the patent application. Here on Archer's island, they were free from U.S. regulation. Stem cell research here, unlike in the States, was given a free hand. There was no need to use stem cells from mice or pigs, as was being done in the U.S. In-vitro fertilization gone bad, aborted fetuses, stillborn children - the supply of stem cells for research was interminable. And other countries like North Korea, China and India were years ahead of the U.S. Yet the formula for recreating a human organ that the body would not reject had eluded the research team thus far. "I see," Dr. Cho said, softly at first, then louder. "I see." It was not simply the process of identifying any semblance of the diseased cells that are then removed from the growing organ that had eluded them. "Yes…yes" Dr. Cho began speaking to himself, in an inaudible mumble, until Archer interrupted him.

"What is it?!? Can you do it?

"I believe we can", Dr. Cho replied. "They have added an isolated enzyme. It's called CDH-2329-Alpha, which acts as a catalyst and stimulates the healthy cells to assist in eliminating diseased cells - that was the key. Assist the body in doing the work of healing itself."

"Do you have what you need?" Archer asked. "Yes," Dr. Cho responded patiently. "In a patent application, they must explain the process such that anyone skilled in the 'art', any bio-chemical engineer worth his degree, should be able to recreate the process. That is why they protect your invention for 20 years, because at the end of the protection period, the public is able to access your patent and anyone who is able, can use your idea."

"Twenty years!" Archer almost yelled. "I don't have twenty years. We need to be able to replace an organ yesterday! How long will it take you?"

Again Dr. Cho demonstrated patience. "With the cell reproduction rate, we should be able to have a prototype available in a few weeks."

"What do you mean a few weeks!? What are all of these little red pulsating pieces of matter floating around in here? Aren't they good for anything? Do you mean to suggest that all of your prior research has been for nothing?"

Doctor Cho sensed a threat in Archer's question. Archer had been very generous to Doctor Cho. He dared not say that he did not have at least one specimen amongst the many that was available to attempt the procedure.

"Certainly, Mr. Archer. I only assumed that you would want us to begin anew, using newly harvested stem cells so that we may monitor the action of the enzyme closely. With the more developed specimens that you see here in the laboratory, we could test their success using some of the locals."

"No," Archer said, more calmly now. "We're not going to waste time on any local islander." Archer was thinking about his son. He had argued with Jill over whether this was the right thing to do. His wife... ex-wife, was dead set against the idea of using her son as a guinea pig. In fact, she was dead set against using embryos to harvest the cells. Jill was a religious woman, and she and her church had thought that using embryos and aborted fetuses to harvest stem cells was an abomination. Archer chuckled to himself. "Dead set against it," he thought. Truer words were never spoken. Archer's boys were now here on the island with him, and, after all of the money and the experimental treatments his youngest son, Brandon, had gone through, he would finally be healed. There was another thought buzzing around in the back of Archer's head, a thought that excited him even more. He knew that he now held the key to not only his own immortality, but riches beyond belief. "We'll see what the priests had to say about it when they were facing death,"

Archer thought to himself. They'd plead with him to give them life, and he would become their god.

"No Doctor, you will have a viable specimen prepared as soon as possible. When we are ready to merge the subject's cells into the stem cells, we will be merging my son Brandon's cells."

"But Mr. Archer, as a scientist I must advise you of the risks and possible consequences of such action. There are myriad possibilities for failure. Some things we may not be able to foresee. This is a completely new . . . ."

"Enough! Archer barked. "This is my responsibility. You'll do as you're told. Notify me as soon as we are ready to merge the cells. I will have Brandon ready."
With that, Archer turned and left the room. You could barely hear the clicking of the soft leather soles of his shoes against the white tiles. He was heading to see Brandon, his youngest, and weakest, son. "Just like his mother", Archer thought. But Archer would fix that now. He would make Brandon into an Archer! Either that or he would die trying. Brandon was nothing like Jason, his first-born. Jason was smart, athletic, good looking, he was HIS son. Sometimes he wondered whether Brandon was an illegitimate child. He was probably weak because his mother was weak.

That's why she turned to drugs. That kind of dependence is only possible in people who are not strong enough to control themselves. Weak people. That was something that Archer never understood. Whatever the reason, Archer was going to make things right. And if things went well for Brandon, Archer would be certain that he too could have a new heart. Sure, he was in great shape, but with a new heart he could be almost super-human. And why stop at a heart? He could use a brand new liver too. Hell, with all of the single malts he'd consumed over the years, he was sure he could use a brand new liver. "I wonder how it would work with the lungs." The wheels were turning. Cigars and scotch were a wonderful combination, and although he was a frequent cigar smoker he knew the effects of tobacco use. Archer was almost in another world now, thinking of all of the possibilities, and all of the money he would make.

Chapter 6

Moments in time were displayed like individual captions as Sarah regained consciousness. Her heart was beating at an accelerated pace, fighting to compete with the pounding in her head. She was freezing deep down in her bones. A steady gush of cold wind seeped through the broken window above her. As she attempted to rub her arms she discovered that she was unable to do so because her hands were bound securely behind her back. Immediately, a kaleidoscope of questions filled her mind - where was she, who tied her up? Who had done this to her and why.

She was lying on her side. The carpeted floor was dingy and heavily soiled, with a musty odor that curled her stomach. The room was dimly lit. The desk in front of her contained stacks of loose paper scattered everywhere. The metal filing cabinet in the corner was more rust than metal. Her arms begin to ache. The position she lay in was extremely uncomfortable. While repositioning her head and shoulder she continued to explore her surroundings. There was a chair to her right. Dark muddied boots anchored both sides of the chair. Sarah held onto the scream that threatened to erupt from the back of her throat, as she was unceremoniously yanked from her prone position and seated upright on the floor.

They were face to face. Silence filled the room. Sarah took measure of Marconi. He was sitting on the chair in front of her, staring. She recognized his eyes. They were the eyes of the monsters that used to hide in her closet as a child, black fathomless orbs that devoured you whole. Sarah held her breath for what seemed an eternity.

Then the monster spoke "Can you keep a secret?"

Sarah blinked repeatedly, wondering if she were sleepwalking through some bizarre nightmare. After a bit of thought she slowly exhaled then decided to answer, "I have never betrayed a confidence". This declaration should have elicited a response, but none came. There was only silence. As the minutes stretched by, her fear began to diminish. "Communications between a client and attorney in furtherance of obtaining legal advice is privileged. My commitment to this rule is solid. I've never been asked to pass such an extreme test before."

Marconi actually smiled. Something he rarely did. This woman was brave and smart. She sat before him armed with nothing more than her wits and courage. Still, he would have to deal with her very carefully. When that fool Thornton told Marconi that his co-worker Sarah Davenport had been eavesdropping on his conversation and overheard everything, Marconi knew he had to act quickly. It took some finessing to distract that police detective long enough to grab Sarah out of her apartment without being spotted. He doubted that she'd had the time to tell him anything. He would soon find out. "Thornton assures me that you are great at keeping secrets".

Huge waves of relief washed through Sarah, calming her anxious imaginings. This was about Thornton, not Mrs. Archer's murder. Whatever this man wanted with her she could deal with. She was safe. That is, as reasonably safe as one could be after being kidnapped right from underneath a cops very nose. Maybe she wasn't so safe after all. A person would have to be pretty desperate to do something like that. Sarah decided to forgo the flippant remark she was about to make, instead opting for a more straightforward approach. "Thornton's secrets are his to tell, not mine."

"I'm glad to hear that Ms. Davenport. My business associates and I can't afford to have you going to the police or anyone else with the information that Thornton so unwisely thought to share." Marconi's eyes locked onto Sarah like the scope of a snipers weapon centered on its target. "What did you tell the detective?"

"Nothing," Sarah said. "I said nothing to him about Thornton. He was there on another matter." Sarah's gaze was unwavering.

Marconi was good at reading people. He had won many poker hands simply by recognizing a bluff when he saw one. He removed the four-inch switchblade from his waste band, noting Sarah's startled gasp as he cut the rope that bound her wrist. He believed her.

"You're free to go Ms. Davenport. Free to continue with your life as though this event never took place," Marconi said as he pulled her to her feet. He noticed that her arms where small yet quite firm. He was pleased that he had no cause to damage such fine bones

Sarah could not believe how abruptly she was being released. She quickly made her way to the door, and then paused as she reached for the handle. She turned and said, "So that's it, no dire word of warning, no ominous threats."

Again Marconi smiled. "No need. I know you'll keep your mouth shut about me and Thornton."

"What makes you so sure", Sarah said

Marconi reached into his jacket pocket. Sarah thought he was going for a gun. She berated herself for not leaving when she had the chance. Even as a child she could never leave well enough alone. Her insatiable curiosity was going to be the death of her yet. Poised to take cover she hesitated as he withdrew - not a gun, but what appeared to be a photograph. He held the photograph, picture side facing her. Sarah was able to focus in on the image. A knot began to form in the pit of her stomach. Beads of moisture appeared out of nowhere across her forehead. It was a picture of Christina, the one she kept in her wallet. It was a picture of her sister.

****

After Sarah disappeared, Jake spent several hours canvassing her neighborhood trying to find some clue as to her whereabouts. One of her neighbors, an elderly woman who lived above her, claimed to have seen Sarah being carried out by a man. When Jake attempted to get a description of this man, the woman invited him in and began to provide details. It did not take long for Jake to realize that the details were much too specific, such as the color of his eyes, the type of cologne that he wore, and the birthmark behind his left ear. When Jake asked the woman if she knew who the man was, she told him that she'd been married to him for fifty-five years before he left to be with the Lord.

The entire search was futile.

Jake was able to board up Sarah's broken window. He cleaned up the glass in the living room and left a message for Sarah on the kitchen table. He asked that she contact him and left each of his numbers; work, home, and cell. Jake then notified the precinct officers about what had occurred and requested that a house watch be placed on Sarah's unit. He wanted to be contacted immediately if they turned up any information on her whereabouts.

Jake could think of nothing else to do, so he decided to visit Archer. In spite of his alibi, Jake considered him to be a suspect in his wife's murder. He may not have killed her himself, but he could easily have paid someone else to do it. Archer's housekeeper answered the door and advised Jake that her employer was not at home. Jake asked when Archer would be home, and the housekeeper replied that he would not be returning this evening, and in fact was out of the country. Jake was hardly surprised that Archer ignored his request not to leave town. Nothing that man did would surprise Jake. However, it didn't appear as if Archer had anything to do with Sarah's disappearance.

Jake decided to spend his time looking for Mrs. Archer's drug connection. Eric had agreed to meet him at Hal's Pub, a little dive on the west end of town. It had been six years since he and Eric had last worked together. They had both been assigned to a specially-created Narcotics task force aimed at cracking down on neighborhood street buys. Jake was always disturbed by the fact that the department never seemed to go after the big money dealers, those responsible for bringing the drugs into the city. The primary focus was the average street hustler, who upon arrest was replaced by another just like him faster than they could process the paperwork. Jake finally had enough when he purchased a rock of crack cocaine off of a nine-year-old boy. He decided then that undercover work was not for him. Too much deceit involved. Too many kids trying to make a living the only way they knew how. He wanted the bad guys to know when he was coming after them and why. So after spending a year in Narcotics and a short stint in Burglary, he transferred to the Homicide division where it seemed he'd found a home.

"Hey buddy, good to see you." Jake said, as he sat down in the booth across from Eric. Jake could tell as they shook hands that Eric was still spending a lot of time in the gym pumping iron. "How are Amy and the kids?"

"Amy and I have been divorced for almost a year now. I hardly ever see the girls. Work keeps me so busy. I had to pick up a special duty job just to cover my child support." Eric shrugged as he said this, but Jake detected a hint of bitterness in his tone. "How about you, you still seeing that pretty gal you brought to the police picnic last summer?

"No, Melanie and I called it quits. She wanted more from me than I had to give." As soon as Jake said it, he knew that it wasn't true. The truth of the matter was that he had it to give he just was unwilling to give it, at least not to her. Immediately Sarah's image flashed across his mind.

"You said on the phone that you were interested in talking to an informant who could connect you with someone dealing in pain killers. I think that I can help you, but my guy won't meet with anyone but me." Eric was suddenly all business. After Jake walked him though the particulars Eric promised to get back with him.

It was late, Jake was tired and frustrated by the time he returned to his apartment. He hadn't eaten since this morning and pulled a slice of cold pizza from the fridge. As he plopped down on the sofa he noticed the red message light on his answering machine. He hoped it was Sarah.

71

Jake hit play. "Hello, Detective Reed, it's me Sara Davenport. I'm home. I'm sorry if you were worried. The last couple of days have just been too much for me. I wasn't thinking clearly at the time. When the bullet came though my window, I only thought to run. Now I can see that I overreacted. I'm sure that it was probably just a stray bullet, but nothing like that has ever happened to me, and my neighborhood is very safe, or at least I thought it was. I guess to put it into police lingo, maybe it was an accidental discharge. Thanks for cleaning up the glass and boarding up my window. You have been so kind to me. First thing tomorrow I am going to send your chief a letter commending your dedication and professionalism. Maybe we can continue where we left off at your convenience" The machine clicked off.

Jake could hardly believe his ears. She'd been missing for hours and all she could say was that she was sorry that she had worried me. It wasn't so much what she said that had him frustrated, but her nonchalant attitude. Her message explained nothing, and left him feeling like he'd been brushed off. As late as it was, he had a mind to drive to her place and demand a better explanation than the one she provided. Jake thought for a moment about why he was so frustrated at the message. He liked this girl. He felt that they had a connection, and he thought the feeling was mutual. He felt that he was entitled to more of an explanation. He thought about the message again. At least she had mentioned continuing…what was it, he replayed the message. Yes, continuing where we left off. He was tired, and probably reading too much into the message. Thinking about it, Sarah was also probably tired. He could wait. Confident and determined that tomorrow he would get some answers.

Chapter 7

Archer returned to the beach house and came upon Jason and Brandon together, as they were most of the time. They were out back in the warm ocean water. Jason was holding Brandon up in the water so he could feel what it might be like to be able to swim. "No kicking." Jason said. "You know you shouldn't exert yourself."

Archer would have to be extra careful when he explained to Jason what was about to happen. Jason and Brandon were extremely close. Jason had watched over Brandon all his life.

Archer walked in through the beach house, ignoring Pearl, his Jamaican housekeeper. Arriving in the back of the house, he walked past the pool and over to the edge of the steps that led to the beach. "Jason, Brandon, I need to see you."

He watched as Jason carefully led Brandon in from the warm ocean water, up the beach. As the boys arrived, Archer ushered them over to the back patio and the boys took a seat. "I have great news. We're finally going to be able to get you that new ticker, Brandon. I've just left Dr. Cho, and he assures me that in a matter of weeks we'll be ready to fix you up better than ever."

Brandon's eyes lit up. He had always wanted to be stronger, to make his father happy. He knew how much his Dad wanted him to be strong like Jason, and he too wanted to be strong. "Really Dad?" Brandon said. Then he coughed, and very subtly he could see the look on his Dad's face turn to disappointment. Just as quickly Archer caught himself and responded with a slight smile "That's right son, it will require a very minor procedure initially, and then, in a week, maybe two, we'll be ready to give you a brand new heart."

Jason looked on, expressionless. He had questions, but didn't want to alarm Brandon, so he'd wait until he could speak to his father alone. He had seen his brother suffer through all of the different experimental treatments over the years, only to be left weaker and more disillusioned about his chances of ever being able to live a normal life. He knew that his father wanted Brandon to be stronger, to be better, and he did not question his father's motives, but he wanted to be sure that this time things would work. He felt Jason squeeze his hand, and his thoughts returned to the present.

"So what I want is for you two to stay here for a couple of more days, and tomorrow I think that Dr. Cho will want to see you Brandon, for a very short procedure."

"What about Mom's funeral?" Brandon asked.

"We'll leave in two days. All of the arrangements have been made; she'll be buried alongside your Grandmother and Grandfather in the family plot. I know you boys miss your mother, we all do. But we have to move on as a family. Your mother would want us to." With that, Archer turned and left the patio.

****

Sarah was upset beyond words. She was pissed! That little weasel Thornton had somehow managed to drag her, and worse still her baby sister, into his quagmire. She couldn't wait to get her hands on Thornton. She thought back to that first night, when Thornton called her house with his absurd accusations - that she was eavesdropping on his conversation. Thornton had probably been talking to the thug who kidnapped her on the other end of the line that night in the office. It had to be him, or someone with whom he was associated. What was it that the thug had said… "me and my associates". Come to think of it, this guy was anything but crazy. A slight chill ran through Sarah's spine. What scared Sarah most is that the guy didn't seem crazy. Recalling the short conversation she had with Marconi, he seemed unnervingly calm about what he was doing, almost self-assured. Sarah thought to herself: "Well, we'll see about that!"

And what about Jake. She had been fortunate that he wasn't at home when she called and she was able to leave a message without much of an explanation. Should she tell him what was really going on? It seemed like the right thing to do. But he seemed to be first and foremost a police officer. He would probably put into motion all kinds of protective measures, including some sort of protective custody for her and her sister. Sarah would be forced to live her life in a shell. And for how long? Could Jake and the rest of the police force really protect her and her sister? After all, she had been kidnapped right in front of Jake. No, she couldn't tell Jake what had happened. Not just yet. She needed to see Thornton and try and figure out what was really going on. After all, why would this guy need a patent? He was no scientist. And while he did seem to be pretty smart, he was more of a muscle-man. He certainly knew how to pull off her kidnapping, and he also knew how to keep her quiet. He was no dummy. He knew what he was doing and he did it well. But he was no scientist. So who was this guy working with, or working for? Who were his associates? She'd have to talk to Thornton. Maybe this sniveling idiot knew more than he had let on. But first she'd have to figure out what she was going to say to Jake. Whatever she did or did not tell him, she still wanted to get to know him better. Besides, it couldn't hurt to have a strong, attractive police officer nearby, whatever happened.

Sarah thought briefly about her sister, and whether she should warn Christina to be careful, but what exactly should she be careful about? Sarah knew only that this thug knew Thornton, and suspected that she knew about this patent, and that Thornton had divulged the patent to this thug and, presumably, his associates, whoever they were. No, she would not say anything to Christina right now. She needed to talk to Thornton.

****

Thornton had tried to go back to work, but he was afraid. He knew that Marconi suspected that he had spilled his guts to Sarah, even though he had lied and said that he had told her nothing. He needed to get away. He was in need of comforting, if only for a night. He only had a couple thousand dollars, but he would have to make do with that. He couldn't go to Marconi for cash. He had gotten into enough trouble with Marconi as it was.

Thornton told his boss that there had been a sudden death in the family and that he needed a few days off. He then caught the next plane to Las Vegas. Thornton loved Vegas. Thornton knew that whatever he did there was his business. He chuckled a bit, as he recalled that runaway bride who was turned over to the authorities by a casino employee, and the employee was later fired. The employee should have kept his mouth shut. Confidentiality in Vegas was sacred. It was the law.

Thornton headed straight for the casino, to the craps table. For the first time in days he felt comfortable. His first roll was an eleven, and two thousand dollars turned into four. His next roll was a seven, and four thousand turned into eight. Mercedes was quick to spot a mark, and she moved in, positioning herself on Thornton's right side, as close as she could get to him without disrupting his throwing motion. She had done this many times before. Thornton noticed her moving in. He was getting excited. The next roll was a four, and the few people who were around the table let out an ominous grunt, knowing that li'l Joe from Kokomo was hard to come by. The next roll was a six. Thornton was sweating by now. It didn't take much for the overweight gambling fiend to perspire. He shook the dice, blew on them once, shoved them in the face of Mercedes and commanded she give 'em a blow. She complied, and he let 'em fly down the table. What seemed like an eternity passed before the first die came to a stop. A one. Thornton knew he still had hope. A four, five or six would have closed the door on this roll. The other die spun on its axis and finally spun out, over against the wall of the craps table, and bounced back next to the other die, tilted, and stopped, slowly falling on its side. A three. A couple of the bystanders clapped a little. Thornton stood there, his eyes gleaming. Thornton had sixteen thousand dollars in less than five minutes, and Mercedes was whispering in his ear and rubbing his thigh. Thornton looked at Mercedes, and looked back at the chips. Mercedes moved her hand up the inside of Thornton's thigh just a bit higher than Thornton expected. Thornton let out a yelp and flung the dice out onto the table. One die rolled along the bottom of the table and stopped at the back wall - a one. The other die bounded off of the table high into the air and bounced off of the back wall. Thornton had a look of utter shock. He had not intended to throw the dice. Snake eyes and it was all over. No Mercedes, no high roller suite, no nothing! At this very moment he didn't know whether he loved Mercedes or hated her. The die bounced and rolled and teetered between a two and a six, finally plopping down with the six facing upward. He hit! Thirty-two thousand dollars! Now he had a glitter in his eyes. He was drunk with excitement. This was why he loved this life. Mercedes was not one to let an opportunity like this slip away. She too knew that Thornton was one roll of the dice away from being just another loser. Recognizing the look in his eyes, she used her head to motion to Porschia. As quickly and as deftly as an ordinary housecat, Porschia positioned herself on Thornton's other shoulder, stroking the hair on the back of his neck. Thornton now recalled the other thing he loved about this life, turning his head to give Porschia a big wide grin, and then back to Mercedes, he scooped up his chips and turned with the two women and headed off into temporary bliss.

****

Archer was getting restless. He knew he was close. Before now it all seemed like a distant dream, now, he was only a couple of months away from holding the key to everlasting life! He could hardly contain his enthusiasm. He was in his office talking on the telephone with Doctor Singh in Mumbai, India. India was another country that was forging ahead with stem cell research and organ development. They were discussing recent developments in England, where scientists were attempting to create human embryos from three genetic parents. Doctor Singh was explaining that the problem with the mitochondrial DNA was that it carries defects in a large amount of the human population. The goal of the researchers was to eliminate the defects in mitochondria. The process, as Archer understood it, was to place the genetic DNA of two parents from an embryo with potentially defective mitochondrial DNA into an embryo that has its genetic DNA removed, but that has healthy mitochondrial DNA. The result was a healthy human with the genetic DNA of two parents, but without the defects of the parents.

Archer was fascinated. While hardly understanding mitochondrial DNA or genetic DNA, Archer had extrapolated this line of thinking into the suggestion that any defects could be "siphoned" from any process where one was creating an organ, or, in this instance, a human being. Remove the bad, and combine the good with the good. Archer's only concern was with his own possible benefits: immortality; power and wealth beyond his imagination. And whatever they were doing in England that helped him reach his goal was great. To hell with some freak kid created in a lab and placed into a womb. If a heart could be constructed from stem cells and the cells from the donee combined with the constructed stem cells so as to be a part of the end product which would eliminate rejection of the organ by the recipient, then why not increase the likelihood of success in the organ by using only the best cells available. Even if those cells had to come from more than two sources.

The wheels were turning now. Archer was envisioning the different product lines he would offer to the world. He would become the owner of the world's first, biggest and best, organ store. Everything depended, of course, upon the price one was able to pay for a new organ. Those with unlimited cash flow could receive the very best "top shelf" organs, those as free from defects as was possible. Those on a more limited budget would not be restricted from receiving a new organ; after all, he was an American. They simply could not afford to be as selective. He also wondered how he could develop maintenance plans for the various product lines. After all, there were huge margins in maintenance.

The more Archer thought about how close he was to a new heart, the more anxious he became. "Is there any way we can speed up the process?" Archer often maintained more than one "expert" on his payroll. He was never the trusting type, and while Doctor Cho was an expert in his field, and Korea had advanced leaps and bounds beyond the United States in this area, Archer knew that there were always different opinions, and therefore different approaches and possibly different results to be gleaned. Just then there was a knock at the door. Archer turned and there was Jason, obviously wanting to have a talk with his father.

"I'll have to call you back, Doctor."
Archer turned and beckoned Jason to come in.

"What's on your mind, son?"

Chapter 8

The next morning Sarah called Maggie, her secretary, and had her put the call through to Thornton. His out-of-office phone message said that he was out attending to family matters and that he would return in three days. Sarah wondered whether Thornton's mom had taken a turn for the worse.

Sarah also wanted to see Jake. They had made plans for dinner, and she wanted to follow through. She decided to give Detective Reed a call.

****

Jake had several other homicides to work. The city was as dangerous as ever. He had just sat down with his morning coffee and folders of the latest four victims of violent death in the city. He sometimes wondered whether the killers would kill themselves off at some point, but there was always a new twist out there, a new drug, a new dealer, a new scam, an old debt, an old grudge or an old flame. He wondered what it was this time. As he sipped his coffee the phone rang. He sat there pondering the matter and finally answered it on the fourth ring.

"Detective Reed, its Sarah Davenport."

"Well, this is a pleasant surprise. Are you OK?"

"Yes. I'm really sorry that I ran off the way that I did. I panicked."

"Don't worry, Sarah, panic is sometimes a good thing. It invokes our fight or flight syndrome, and I guess this time your instinct was the latter." he chuckled.

Sarah knew that she was being overly sensitive, but found it hard just then to appreciate the jest. "It's bad enough that you think I'm a coward, but to laugh about it as well …."

"Now hold on Sarah." Jake sat his coffee mug on the table and sat upright.

His tone became softer when Sarah said, "I didn't mean to offend you. In the short period of time we've been acquainted I've had a chance to examine some of your more outstanding attributes. Courage is at the top of the list."

Jake's words had their desired effect, comforting Sarah. His opinion was important to her. She wanted to tell him that she hadn't run, but was forced from her apartment. However, the risk to her sister outweighed his good opinion of her.

When Sara remained silent Jake continued, "Look I was just remembering the first time anybody took a shot at me. I was one scared guy. Fortunately for me, my partner

Steve was one cool customer. He grabbed me and pulled me down behind the car door and told me to sit tight. He went around to the other side of the car and had a clear shot at the perp. He popped him in the knee dropping him to the ground, causing him to release the weapon. Before I knew it, Steve moved in and had the guy cuffed. I was caught off guard. More shocked than afraid. It was so sudden. These things always seem to happen when you least expect. No, I wasn't laughing at you, I was laughing at myself."

While the thought of Sarah taking off amused him, he certainly did not want her to think that he would laugh at her, at least not until he knew her better. Some women can take being laughed at, and sometimes would even laugh at themselves, but some could not. He hoped Sarah was the former. He had sensed that she was a self-assured woman, it was one of the things that drew him to her, and he hoped that he had not read her wrong.

"And please, Sarah, call me Jake."

"Alright" Sarah said, and then paused for effect, "Detective Jake Reed it is. As I recall, the last time we spoke, we had agreed to dinner."

"I believe you are correct Madam. I should get off tonight at around 7:00, how's 8:30?"

"Sounds good to me."

"Great. I'll see you then."

"Bye Jake."

Jake could hear her smile on the other end of the line. "See you later, Sarah."

****

Jason wanted nothing more than for Brandon to be healthy and strong. He knew his father wanted the same thing. But he kept hearing his mother's voice, saying how it was morally wrong to sacrifice one life to save another. It didn't matter to her that the life to be saved was her son's, and his brothers. She would say that God would take care of Brandon, just as he had done so far. She felt that no good could come from men experimenting with life the way they were, pretending to be God. It was wrong, and evil, and someday God would have his revenge. One of the things Jason really appreciated about his mother was that she was principled. She always used to say that "if you don't stand for something, you'll fall for anything."

Jason also knew that his father didn't really believe in God. And while his father would never come right out and say it, he never put faith in anything other than the almighty dollar and himself. Jason could recall the days when his parents would argue over treatment options for Brandon. Those were fierce arguments, and he hated when they argued.

"Son?"

"Yes father, I was wondering about the new heart Brandon is getting. Will this really work? I mean, he's been through a lot, and every time you promised that he'd get better. The treatments take a lot out of him." What Jason didn't say was that it took a lot out of him too.

"Don't worry son. This time it's a sure thing. In fact, I just left the doctor's office before coming to break the news to you and Brandon. I personally reviewed the procedure." Archer wanted to add that he was so sure of the process that he too was in line for a transplant, but he thought better of it.

Jason suspected that this had something to do with the arguments his parents had just days before his mom's death, but he was reluctant to raise the issue with his father. Instead, he simply said "I just want to be sure."

"We all do, son. If you'd like, I'll take you to see the doctor tomorrow, and you can see for yourself, O.K.?"

Jason's eyes lit up. "Brandon too?" He was ever mindful of his younger brother.

"Sure."

With that, Jason turned and left the room. He still had his doubts, but maybe things would work out OK despite all that had happened.

Archer returned to his thoughts of immortality. "Hormones! Doctors fed hormones to livestock; hell, they even prescribed hormones to kids to help them grow. Maybe that was the answer to speeding up the growth process." He picked up the phone and dialed Doctor Singh. He figured he'd run the idea past Doctor Singh before taking it to the sometimes too damned careful Doctor Cho.

****

Jake knew it was a bad idea to date a witness involved in an active case. Not only did his instincts warn against it, but it was common knowledge within the Force that getting involved with a witness or a victim, or anyone involved in a case that was pending was bad news. One could not help but become emotionally involved, which would inevitably lead to biased judgment. And although the possibility was remote, Sarah could in fact be the murderer. Jake knew this was far-fetched, but he also knew that it was possible. Getting involved with Sarah would make the possibility, at least to him, more remote. This could even be a part of some coolly calculated plan of Sarah's to gain his confidence and thus

90

throw him off of her trail. Everything about this was wrong. At the same time, he knew that he was only being a cop, and there was no way that Sarah was involved in the murder of Mrs. Archer. Face it, she really is a wonderful person. Jake knew that women like Sarah didn't come along every day. He'd be crazy not to take her out on a date. He had to follow through with this, if only to see where it took him. She was a great girl, and Jake owed it to himself not to let this opportunity pass him bye.

It was 6:30 and Jake was wrapping up some paperwork, preparing to head home and prepare for his date. He had butterflies thinking about it. That was something Jake hadn't felt in a long time. He realized again that he really liked this woman. Sarah was special.

Before leaving, Jake placed a call to Eric. He didn't think that Eric would have had anything yet. It's only been a couple of days, but he figured that it was worth a phone call. Eric was out. Jake left a message and headed home.

****

Sarah decided to make one last attempt to reach Thornton. She called Maggie back and asked her to get Thornton's address. Maggie knew Thornton's secretary, or Administrative Assistant as they want to be called these days, and had no trouble getting Thornton's address. After retrieving the information Sarah headed over to Thornton's apartment just in case he had come home. Thornton lived in a high-rise building in the older part of town. Sarah thought that he would have lived in a nicer place, given his salary, but Thornton obviously had issues that she knew nothing about.

Sarah entered the lobby and walked past the doorman, who looked up and was more interested in "checking Sarah out" than checking Sarah in. She walked over to the elevator and pressed the up button. Arriving on the eighth floor, Sarah checked the numbers and headed left, to 812. Sarah rang the buzzer. No answer. She rang it again and listened for any sounds coming from inside. Nothing. Maybe Thornton did go to visit his mother. Sarah turned to leave. Just then, the door across the hall opened, and an elderly woman stuck her head out peering over the rim of her bifocals.

"He left yesterday"

"Excuse me?"

"He left yesterday. He wasn't carrying much of anything, but he hasn't returned yet."

Sarah wasn't sure what to say. "I was wondering how his mother was doing.

Thornton said that she was ill and that he needed to check on her."

"His mother? No dear, you must be mistaken. Thornton's mother passed away several years ago." The woman pushed her bifocals further up the bridge of her nose to get a better look at Sarah. Upon further inspection she replied, "Had she been alive Thornton probably would not have bothered to check on her. They had a very strained relationship. He resented the fact that she lived in some big fancy house while he could only afford this place. One would think with him being an attorney and all that he could afford to do better. He was quite disappointed to discover that his mother had not left him a dime."

Sarah was briefly taken-a-back. It must have showed on her face.

"I'm sorry dear. I wasn't going to say anything, but you look like a nice girl, not like the others."

Again Sarah was caught off guard. Thornton had girlfriends, more than one.

"It's not that the other girls aren't well dressed, but they look like professionals to me. You know what I mean. I can spot 'em, even the high class ones"

Sarah was starting to feel a bit apprehensive. "I'm sorry. I'm just a co-worker and I was concerned when Thornton didn't come into work."

"Oh, are you a lawyer too?"

"Yes Ma'am."

"Well, you look like a real nice girl, someone who would be good for Thornton. I worry about him. He seems to be so lonely. Thornton doesn't talk to me that often but when he does I'm happy to listen. I don't think he has anybody else to confide in"

"I'm sure that you are a great comfort to him", Sarah said as she smiled at the older woman. "Well, I guess I should be on my way."

"Would you like to have some tea?"

"No thank you, Ma'am. I really should be going."

"O.K, I'll be sure to tell Thornton you came by."

Sara was afraid she would. But to suggest that she shouldn't might raise suspicion. So she again thanked the lady and left. She didn't know quite what to make of Thornton. Sarah exited the building and flipped open her cell phone. Since she had the day off she may as well check on Christina. She called the hospital, but Chris was at a seminar and would be out for the day.

Sarah decided to spend a relaxing day at the spa. She got the works - manicure, pedicure and full body massage. She had no idea where Jake was planning on taking her tonight. She was so relaxed she felt like she could even ballroom dance without tripping over her feet. Sarah had taken a few dance lessons but had not quite mastered the intricate footwork of ballroom dances. Arriving home, she rummaged through her closet and finally decided on her little black dress. It had spaghetti straps and complimented her figure, falling just above her knees. It was appropriate for any event. Or so it had seemed.

She soon discovered her error when Jake arrived strolling through the door wearing blue jeans and sneakers. This was not what Sarah had expected. Until now she had only seen Jake in a suit, and had assumed he would be similarly dressed this evening. Of course after wearing a suit to work all day it only made sense that he would want to be more comfortable during his off time. Sarah could not help but notice how superbly the jeans hugged his thighs. The cut was perfect for his muscular physique. There were definite benefits to going casual.

Jake's appearance may not have been what Sarah expected, but Sarah's appearance was just what Jake had expected. She looked gorgeous from head to toe. Jake had considered calling her on the way over to tell her to dress casually, but as she stood before him he was glad he hadn't.

"Just give me a minute to change",
Sarah said as she headed for her bedroom.

"NO!" Jake shouted reaching out to
grab her arm before she could make a hasty
retreat. He gently spun her around, looking
her straight in the eyes. "Not the dress." Jake
looked at her with undisguised passion, "Just
the heels. You will need comfortable shoes for
what I have in mind." Jakes mouth twitched as
he added, "But keep the heels out for later".

Sarah grabbed some comfortable shoes,
and smiled as Jake assisted her with her coat.
"So are you going to tell me where we're
going?"

"Nope", Jake replied with a devilish
gleam in his eye.

Jake was driving a black convertible
BMW. He opened her door and buckled her
in, just as he had that night at the Archers.
Sarah kind of liked being taken care of this
way. It made her feel protected and cherished.
There was soft jazz music playing on the radio.
Sarah loved all kinds of music. Her mother
was a classical pianist who exposed her and
her sister to many styles of music. They would
frequently attend Broadway productions,
operas, and the symphony. Her mom was
gone now. She missed her so much. Thank
God she still had Christina.

The car stopped in front of a sign that
read "Police Firing Range." Sarah turned to

look at Jake who was sporting a huge grin. "Ever shot a gun before?" Jake said as he reached to unbuckle her seatbelt. He got out of the car and came around to help Sarah exit the vehicle.

Sarah was stunned. She had never fired a gun but it was on her list of things to do some day. Before she could reply to Jakes question or even voice an objection, Jake was ushering her inside. When he placed the large metal gun in her hand Sarah almost dropped it. "Wait! The answer to your question is no, I've never held a gun before, much less fired one." Sarah looked as if she were holding a pin-less grenade. "I don't know if I'm ready to do this."

Jake could see that Sarah was not comfortable holding a weapon, that she knew absolutely nothing about guns. He, on the other hand, knew everything there was to know about weaponry. It was one of his many hobbies. He was sure that with a little instruction Sarah would soon master the concept.

"Listen Sarah, I know that this is not your typical first date, but you impress me as the type of woman who needs to know how to shoot. Sometimes trouble finds you, whether you like it or not. Indulge me in this. Who knows, you might just enjoy it."

The range was deserted this time of the evening. The ordinance section had only a skeleton crew working. The Department had no firearms training scheduled this month, which meant the range was open for practice. Jake signed himself and Sarah in at the desk, retrieved a couple of targets, and proceeded into the indoor range. The first fifteen minutes was spent going over gun safety. Jake had Sarah load and unload the gun several times. The thirty-eighty semi-automatic fit nicely in her hand. The Walther PPK was one of his favorite guns. It was also the preferred weapon of James Bond, the greatest action character of all time.

Once Jake explained the process and Sarah became comfortable holding the weapon, she became quite excited about firing it. Sarah could hardly believe she was actually at a police firing range about to shoot a gun. She knew that no matter how the evening turned out she would always be grateful to Jake for allowing her to scratch this from her "bucket list."

"Always remember to point the gun downrange, even when loading and unloading", Jake said as he handed Sarah a gun that was loaded and ready to go.

Sarah took a good stance the way Jake showed her to do, and pointed the gun at the target as Jake had instructed. Before she was ready or even realized what she had done she pulled the trigger. The recoil was greater than expected, and her shot was high and to the right of the center of her target. Before she could get another shot off, Jake wrapped his arms around each of hers. He explained that her shot was off because her grip was too loose. Sarah could feel Jake's' breath on the right side of her neck as he explained "The secret to being a good marksman is grip, breathe control, and trigger squeeze."

This time Sarah gripped the gun firmly, took a deep breath, and slowly squeezed the trigger. There was a hole smack through the center of the silhouette. "Yes!" Sarah exclaimed. Exhilarated, Sarah proceeded to empty her magazine. She never imagined shooting would be such fun.

Jake enjoyed watching her. The way her hips swung back and forth as she positioned herself for her shot. Her body was sleek, yet curvaceous. Not only did she shoot well, but she looked damned great in that dress. Tonight he was going to break a cardinal rule and put off cleaning his gun before he left. He was anxious to move on with the evening.

The Italian restaurant was one of Jake's favorites. The owners knew him by name and had reserved the table by the fireplace as he had requested. There weren't many customers this late in the evening, which contributed to the cozy atmosphere that Jake had in mind.

Sarah had never been to this restaurant, but was pleased by Jake's choice. The food was delicious. The staff was attentive without being intrusive, which gave them an opportunity to converse with minimal interruption. The more she learned about Jake, the more fascinating he became. She liked this man a lot. Unsure if it was the wine or Jake's company, she knew she was becoming intoxicated, knew that when he drove her home she would invite him in, which is exactly what she did when they pulled in front of her place.

"Would you like some coffee?" Sarah asked.

"What I'd like ... is you"

Sexually charged did not adequately describe the tension in the car. Sarah could hardly breathe. Her lips parted as she tried to inhale small bits of air. Jake stared into her eyes reading the response that she could not seem to verbalize. Then he moved. Taking her in his arms he crushed his body against hers. Passion ignited. He devoured her lips, taking possession as his tongue swept inside completely dominating her mouth. Sarah was consumed with need. She returned the kiss with equal fervor, winding her hands around his neck in an unbreakable clinch.

"We'd better take this inside," Jake suggested as he nibbled the corner of her mouth. She tasted so good, and the perfume she was wearing drove him wild. It was hard to stop. It had been many years since he had made out in a car. Somehow he knew that this was not the time to revisit that experience.

Sarah was still reeling from the kiss and did not want to stop, but she could not argue that they should go inside. There was no telling who was watching at this point. She was attempting to reach for the door handle when her cell phone rang. She threw an apologetic look Jake's way as she answered the call. "Dump the cop or your sister dies." As the phone went dead Sarah suddenly lost all control. It was as if a dam had broken. She began to weep incessantly. At first Jake was taken aback. Confused by what had occurred. He repeatedly tried to get Sarah to tell him what was wrong but was unable to do so. Jake held her as she sobbed in anguish. His passion cooled as his protective instincts took over.

When Sarah was finally able to gain control she did not trust herself to speak. She was afraid that at any moment she would tell Jake everything, placing his life and that of her sister's in danger. It was all too much. Mrs. Archer's murder, being kidnapped, having her sister's life threatened, and getting involved with Jake, all happening so fast. She was an emotional rollercoaster that had peeked and was going down fast. What must Jake be thinking? She hated lying, but there was no way she could tell him the truth. Taking a deep breath, she attempted to pull herself together and come up with a plausible explanation.

"I'm mortified that I broke down like that. It's just that I've received some bad news. There's a family emergency. I'm sorry Jake, but I can't explain right now. I have to attend to this matter." Sarah avoided making eye contact.

"Is there anything I can do?"

"No. Thank you for asking. I'm afraid I have to go," Sarah said as she hopped out of the car.

Jake caught up to her and insisted on walking her to her door. She could tell that he wanted to know more, but before he could say anything else, she said goodnight, giving him a quick kiss on the cheek. Sarah leaned against the door she had just closed in Jakes face. Will this nightmare ever end?

Expecting to hear from her kidnapper, Sarah dozed off on the sofa. When she had awakened, the sun was up. This had to end. Yes, somehow she'd make it end. Knowing that the best defense is a good offense, Sarah decided that she was not going to sit around and wait to be threatened again. She was going to become the aggressor, and she'd start with Thornton.

Chapter 9

Eric sunk the eight ball as Dopp strolled through the door. He grabbed his drink and collected the winnings reluctantly handed to him by his opponent. Making eye contact with Dopp, he proceeded to an isolated corner. Dopp took a few minutes to speak to the bar's regular customers. This place was a second home to many of his fellow cronies. Eric had been patronizing the establishment for several months now, becoming quite the regular himself. His was a familiar face. People in the area had no reason to suspect that he was an undercover cop. He'd been one of them for a while now.

"Words out you looking to score a fix," Dopp whispered to Eric as he slid into the seat beside him.

"Not exactly," Eric said as he leaned in closer to Dopp. "It's not the fix I'm seeking, but the dealer."

The crease in Dopp's forehead deepened as he frowned. Getting Dopp to roll over on the dealer was going to be tougher than Eric had expected. He knew that it was not necessary, but he assured Dopp that the information would not be traced back to him. Even so, Dopp was not as forthcoming as usual. Finally Eric said, "You owe me. Need I remind you that I helped you avoid prosecution when that street bust went bad last month?

"Yeah, well that may be but I don't owe you my life, which is exactly what I'd be risking if word got out that I gave up the Doc."

"The Doc?"

"That's the name he goes by. Word is he used to perform plastic surgery on all the rich and famous, until he got hit with a big malpractice suit. The man's got many connections and many dangerous associates." Dopp slowly shook his head. "There's a big market for prescription drugs, but suppliers are hard to come by, which makes him a protected commodity."

"Look, I'm not looking to take down this Doc fellow or his operation. I just need information concerning a potential customer."

Erik could see that Dopp was considering his request. He decided to push a little harder "It would be a shame if Code Enforcement received a list of the rundown buildings you've been renting out as crack houses."

One of the reasons Dopp had lasted so long in this game was that he attempted to avoid trouble like the plague. In the years he'd known Eric he'd never seen him make an idle threat. He always did what he said he'd do. It was better to have Eric owing him than pursuing him. Plus, Eric always protected his source. Dopp, however, did not want to appear too easy, so he'd make him wait another fifteen minutes or so before giving Eric the information he wanted.

Eric left the bar feeling charged and satisfied. The evening had gone as expected. He loved being a player in this game of cops and robbers. It was a natural high for him. He was addicted. Although he had sacrificed his family, he had no regrets. This job was his life, the life that he wanted. Tonight he'd scored. Mark another one for the good guys. Jake would be pleased.

Chapter 10

There was no response when Sarah called Thornton's home again this morning. At the office she was told that he had taken another vacation day. Sarah was tired of waiting. She went to Thornton's administrative assistant and had her unlock his office door. She told her that she needed to find a file she had left with Thornton last week. No, she did not need assistance in locating it. Once she was in the office Sarah shut the door. She was not sure what she was looking for, but she would look until she found something to shed some light on what it was that Thornton had gotten them both into.

After rifling through two large file cabinets Sarah finally came across a folder marked Jackrabbit, Inc. Jackrabbit was the name of the company that Thornton had mentioned the day he came to see her. Sarah quickly stuck the folder in her briefcase closed the file cabinet and left the office. She went straight to the copy machine down the hall and started copying the file, one hundred and sixty-four pages. It was a heavy duty copier that had all the latest gadgets. It took only minutes and the entire file was copied.

"Hey Sarah, didn't expect you back today." It was Adam. He was walking straight towards her.

Sarah positioned her body in front of the copier, hoping to block the printing that was being done. "Hi Adam, I only came in to take care of some high priority work. You know me, always a team player." The machine stopped.

"Give me whatever you're working on and I'll have Charlie take care of it," Adam said as he held out his hand.

Sarah smiled. A great big dazzling smile as she grabbed a hold of Adam's arm, swinging him away from the copy machine. "Adam, you know how it works around here. This client is a special client, and I'd like to keep him all to myself. I want you to know how much I appreciate you Adam. You have been so wonderful to me since the incident with Mrs. Archer, and I do have a favor to ask: I guess that I am more disturbed by Mrs. Archer's death than I had realized. After I'm done here, I'd like a little more time off to get my head together. I've been thinking about my sister a lot and would like to spend a little time with her."

"Of course" Adam said, patting her hand. "It was a harrowing experience. Naturally you'd be shaken up by it. Don't worry, take whatever time you need, and if there are any more pressing issues that you aren't so protective of, let me know and I can assign your cases to Charlie."

"That would be great. If you don't mind could you talk to him now? I'd like to know that he's OK with it and be able to answer any questions he may have while I'm still here," Sarah said as she uncoiled her hand from around his arm.

As Adam headed back down the hall Sarah swiftly turned, grabbed the papers from the copy machine and stuffed them into her briefcase. She then retraced her steps, putting the original folder back into Thornton's office where she had found it. It turned out to be quite a productive morning. She really did have some important cases that needed immediate attention. A few she handled herself, and the rest she turned over to Charlie.

When she left the office Sarah went to a public library. She wanted to get as much research on Jackrabbit, Inc. as she could find. The file from Thornton's office showed that Jackrabbit had applied for several patents involving stem cells and genetic engineering. Sarah knew next to nothing about stem cells and had to spend several hours researching the topic. There was one particular breakthrough that Jackrabbit was touting involving stem cells and organ production. This was the subject of Thornton's file.

Sarah knew that the government had set strict limits on federal funding for stem cell research. As a result, most stem cell research was being done in the private sector, where it was loosely regulated. Sarah found this to be an ethical minefield. She too did not believe that humans should attempt to play God. Jackrabbit had actually grown a human kidney. The entire process was quite fascinating, and obviously very lucrative. No wonder Thornton's cohorts were so interested in getting their hands on this file, and keeping it secret.

There was much more information in the file, most of which Sarah was not able to understand. She would have to have someone in the medical field review the rest and explain things to her in layman's terms. Maybe she could ask Christina a few questions without getting her involved. Of course, she was already involved, she just didn't know it.

After leaving the library, Sarah headed home. She changed into a jogging suit and took off running. She had so much to think about. Running was the best way she knew to clear her mind. So many things had happened over the last several days that she really had become stressed. She still could not believe how she fell apart last night. What must Jake think of her? Yes, she needed to run. Exercise was the best way to release endorphins, and right now she could use some endorphins.

Sarah ran her usual five miles and felt great. She did a few short cool down exercises, then took a seat on a nearby park bench. A woman came up and sat next to her. She was an older woman who had on far too much perfume and far too little deodorant. She asked Sarah if she could spare a few dollars. Sarah never carried money when she was out running. She apologized to the woman and advised her that she had no money and could not assist her. She felt regret. Sarah could not help but stare at the woman as she walked away. The woman was obviously down on her luck, but in spite of this carried herself with a regal comportment. She had the most striking red hair Sarah had ever seen.

The presence was felt before it was seen. She turned around and there on the bench sitting beside her was the man who had kidnapped her. The thug was actually sitting there, right beside her in the light of day. It was almost dusk but still bright enough for Sarah to see the small whiskered indentations on his face. Sarah immediately turned to call out to the redheaded woman. She was still close enough to hear her if she screamed. It was doubtful, however, that she could be of any real assistance. There were no other people in sight. Sarah turned back to the thug and looked him straight in the eye. She was getting angry. What do you want?

"Nice night for a run," Marconi said as he stared back at Sarah.

Apparently this man had no fear. It was rare for a kidnapper to allow his captive to see his face and live to tell of it. This man had made no attempt to hide his appearance from her, not the first time, and not now. Did he care that she could have him arrested for his crimes? Or was he confident that he could take her out without anyone being the wiser. Whatever his reasons, he was apparently unconcerned that Sarah was able to identify him.

"What exactly is it that you want from me," Sarah said.

"I want you to stay away from the cop," Marconi said in a matter of fact way. "I'm sure you know that I've been watching your place and I'm not real comfortable with the amount of time you've been spending with that police detective. It's only a matter of time before you're tempted to tell him all about me."

"I haven't so far and I won't. I cannot just avoid the police all together. The police have been questioning me about an entirely different matter. It would seem strange if I suddenly cut off all contact."

Marconi considered her reply. She was a lawyer and as such would be in constant communication with law enforcement personnel. He realized that he could not control every contingency. He just needed to ensure Sarah's silence until he could put his plan into effect. "I guess I'll have to take your word for it and trust you to place your sister's welfare above everything else. But know that I'm around... watching... as always."

Before she could respond, he was gone, as quickly and silently as he had appeared. Sarah was no longer afraid. If he wanted to kill her he would have done so by now. If her demise is what he had in mind, opportunities had presented themselves in abundance. However, she knew without a doubt that he would hurt her sister if she ever exposed the information that Thornton had so carelessly revealed to her.

Sarah was not feeling quite so relaxed anymore. She considered going for another run but it was beginning to get dark. She needed to get home. Mrs. Archer's funeral was tomorrow and she planned to attend the service. In addition to handling her divorce, she had also drafted a new will for Mrs. Archer. Mrs. Archer had a previously existing will at the time she asked Sarah to represent her. However, she made it clear that her husband's attorney had written it for her at her husband's request, and she wanted to have her own say as to whom she would be leaving her possessions. Sarah knew that Mr. Archer was in for a surprise during the probate proceedings. That was just one more thing Sarah was not looking forward to.

Chapter 11

The sun would not rise for another hour. Marconi was just getting home. He went to the bar and poured a drink, and then to the balcony. He thought back to his days in the orphanage. No one wanted to adopt the short, stocky kid with the bad attitude. His dark olive skin didn't help his chances. Marconi learned early that it was far better to just not give a damn what anyone else thought.

His first lesson came early on when he was rejected by the first of many nice, upper middle class couples who came to find their little bundle of joy. He told himself then that the rest of the world could kiss his ass. And each time he was passed over for adoption this attitude was reinforced; strengthened. Instead of retreating into a shell and feeling sorry for himself, Marconi got angry. At first he took out his anger on the other children. By the time Marconi was thirteen he was taking on the counselors. Soon he realized that even they, the adults, were afraid of him. When he was fourteen, the criminal justice system began to care for him. Marconi was sent to juvenile detention after he was caught breaking into one of the residences surrounding the orphanage.

On the first day in detention, he was in the cafeteria and had just sat down with his tray, when three boys came over to his table. One of them asked Marconi his name. Marconi glanced over at the boy and half lowered his head, never taking his eyes off of the boys. He knew their intentions were not to befriend him, and he could feel the eyes of the entire cafeteria turned his way. He sized up the boys. The one asking the question was the leader, the apparent brains of this group. He was not the biggest, but neither was he small. The second kid was the muscles. Tall and thick, Marconi knew that he would have to disable him quickly. The third kid was the weakest of the three. He was skinny and almost as short as Marconi. He was the gopher for the group. He'd do whatever the other two said, and when they went down he'd run for cover.

Marconi wanted the element of surprise, and one of the few ways to achieve this in this kind of setting was to make the boys feel overconfident. Marconi was trying to appear to be afraid, and when one of them moved in, Marconi would let loose the fury for which he would become infamous.

"Hey man, don't be scared, we just want to be your friend. After we eat we'll take you around. There are some guys in here who want to put the jelly bug up your butt. Do you know what the jelly bug is?" The skinny kid smiled. The biggest kid sat back. He was too far away for Marconi to make a move. Marconi shook his head no, but continued to look down. On his tray was a plastic fork and spoon. "Don't worry, we'll protect you." The brains then made his mistake. He put his right hand on Marconi's left shoulder and began to rub it. Within seconds Marconi grabbed the fork near its base with his right hand while almost simultaneously turning and grabbing the back of the kids head with his left hand and he rammed the fork into the kids left eye. The big kid witnessed what occurred and was momentarily left in shock as his cohort started screaming at the top of his lungs.

This was the opening Marconi needed. He lunged for the big kids throat and bit into it like a wild animal. The force of Marconi's weight drove the kid back onto a second table. Boys were scrambling to get out of the way, forming a circle around the two combatants. The big kid was wailing away at Marconi, and blood began to flow from his neck. Marconi pulled back and spat into the kids face and followed with a thunderous overhand right that caught the center of his temple, knocking him into a daze. The guards were trying to get through the crowd to get at Marconi. Marconi looked around for the third kid and saw him backing away from the melee. Marconi yelled "come here my friend, I've got something for you!" Marconi issued a loud roar and sprung like a wild beast towards the kid. The crowd instinctively moved aside. The guards now had a clear path to Marconi, but were hesitant to move in.

Marconi was a sight to see. He had blood on his mouth, chin and his neck, and he was yelling and moving so fast that he was hard to catch, especially when the effort to catch him was half-hearted. Whistles were blowing and kids were screaming, which only added to the adrenaline rushing through Marconi. He loved this. He was in his element. Suddenly out of nowhere a huge counselor grabbed Marconi from behind, tackling him to the ground. The two guards who had been standing in the room quickly rushed over to provide assistance. The three of them were still unable to get Marconi under control or keep him on the ground. Finally one of the guards discharged a taser, set on stun mode, striking Marconi in the groin. He instantly convulsed then fell still. The guards put hand cuffs and leg irons on Marconi and drug him away. Marconi spent one month in isolation, but when he came out, he was on his way to an easy stay in Juvy Hall.

Marconi looked around his lavishly appointed Penthouse apartment, and thought about the Thorntons and the Archers of this world, and felt an air of superiority. They would never understand him. But he knew them, and he knew that he was just as deserving of Archer's money as Archer was. Sure, Archer paid him well, but what he paid was only a fraction of what he could afford. Marconi knew there was something special about the file he had extorted from Thornton, and Marconi wanted in. The sooner he found Thornton the sooner he got answers.

Chapter 12

Thornton was in a deep sleep. He was back in his old bedroom at his mother's house. It was Saturday, which meant that he could sleep in late. But then he heard something... a knock at the door. Faint at first, the knocking grew louder. It was probably his mother demanding that he get up. She always ruined Saturday mornings for him. Still half asleep, Thornton heard the door opening. As he opened his eyes he realized that he was not in his old bed, but in a hotel room. Just then the maid turned the corner and said "Excuse me Sir, I thought the room was empty. I'll come back." Still disoriented, Thornton mumbled an O.K.

He looked around the empty room noting that Mercedes and Porschia were nowhere to be found. He glanced over to the chair where his pants lay draped across the seat, and knew immediately that they had cleaned him out. These were the times he hated most, when he was kicked back into reality. As his memories of the evening returned, he recalled that he was in trouble, and had left work to get away from the whole mess. Now he was broke, and had no place to go. He didn't even have airfare back home. Not that he particularly cared about going back. He crawled out of bed and noticed the hotel bill on the floor near the door. He checked his wrist for his watch, and it too was gone. Dammit! The digital alarm clock display read nine fifty-two. He walked over to the floor and picked up the bill. Check-out was ten o'clock. He picked up the phone and called the front desk. "Hi, this is Mr. Hilliard in room 424, and I'd like to request a late check-out?"

"I'm sorry Mr. Hilliard, but that room is booked for today and we need to have it as soon as possible."

Damn, Thornton thought. "O.K." he said, and hung up the phone. He threw on his socks and pants and shoes. He went into the bathroom and threw some water on his face and in his mouth to get rid of the dry, cottony feel, and then on his head to help lay his hair down into something manageable. He wiped his face with the towel and grabbed his shirt, took one last look around the room to see if there was anything of value that the hookers may have missed. Disappointed, he opened the door and went into the hallway. He ambled past the maid's cart to the elevator and down to the lobby, where he sat in one of the lounge chairs to sort things out. He knew payday was weeks away. The firm paid monthly, and he had spent the only money he had. He thought back to the roll he was on and smiled to himself. He really could be quite the stud. But now he needed money. He thought about calling Sarah with a story that he was kidnapped and robbed. Maybe she'd feel sorry for him and front him some money. No, Sarah was a little edgy the last time they spoke, and she wanted him to go to the police. Now that Marconi had gotten what he wanted he certainly would not be willing to advance any more cash. Thornton's secretary had loaned him money once. He'd even paid her back, so she might be willing to do so again.

Thornton went to the desk and asked to use a phone. "There's a pay phone around the corner near the restroom, Sir." The clerk's inquisitive glance and tone reminded Thornton of his disheveled appearance. He picked up the phone and called Delores collect. She accepted the charges, which was a good sign. However, before Thornton could launch into his story she asked, rather urgently, where he was. She told him that Sarah had come in and went into his office to look for a file. It must have been the Jackrabbit file. She also said that just yesterday a Mr. Marconi had been there looking for him. A chill passed through Thornton. His grip on the receiver tightened. For several heart stopping seconds an uneasy silence remained as Delores waited for his response. Finally, Thornton replied "Oh really, what did Mr. Marconi want?"

"He just asked to see you. I told him that you had a death in the family and would be out of the office for several days. He asked whether I knew where you had gone, and I said that I assumed you went back home to settle your mother's affairs.
Did I do something wrong?"

"Yes you certainly did! How many times have I told you not to give out any personal information about me." Thornton was beside himself. He was more afraid than anything.

"I'm sorry Mr. Thornton, I didn't mean to do anything wrong. I won't let it happen again." Delores' words were laced with regret.

Thornton thought quickly. He needed cash. He dared not alienate Delores, who could be his only salvation. "It's OK Delores. Don't worry about it. It's just that I'm in a bit of a bind. Do you have any money you could loan me? The funeral expenses have all but drained me."

"I have a little, how much do you need this time?"

"Five hundred" Thornton said, peevishly.

"Sure Thornton, I've got that. Do you want me to send you a check?"

"No, I really can't wait on the mail. Could you deposit it into my checking account at my bank? I really appreciate this Delores.

Please don't tell anyone about this, I'm kind of embarrassed about the whole thing."

"Certainly Mr. Hilliard. Give me your account number?"

Yes! Thornton thought. "Thanks Delores. I really appreciate it. I'll pay you back on payday." Thornton provided Delores his account number, and headed to the airport for an ATM and a ticket home.

"When should I say you'll be back?"

"If anyone asks, tell them I'm wrapping things up here and I should be back in a couple of days."

Thornton hung up. Why would Marconi attempt to track him down? What does he want now? Thornton was scared to death of Marconi. It must be Sarah. What had she screwed up this time? Dammit! Why did she have to go snooping around in the Jackrabbit file? Thornton was really terrified. He'd much rather confront Sarah than Marconi. Sarah wanted him to go to the police, but Marconi would not like that at all. Maybe he should see Marconi, and tell him about Sarah's snooping. Marconi would know what to do with Sarah. Then again, maybe he could tell Sarah about Marconi, and she would get the police involved, but then he would go to jail. No, Thornton decided to find Marconi and tell him what Sarah had done. With Sarah out of the way, Thornton would be safe. Thornton went outside to grab a taxi.

Chapter 13

It was a windy day on the Western end
of the island. The water was warm this time of
year, and Brandon wanted Jason to teach him
how to surf. Jason knew that Brandon was not
strong enough to surf. Brandon could barely
swim fifty feet before he was near exhaustion.
Jason, however, could never say no to his little
brother. He had Arie bring up the board, and
headed down the short stretch to the beach.
Jason figured he'd let Brandon ride the board
out on his belly, but no standing today.
Brandon took a few short strokes while Jason
walked beside him. When a wave came along
Jason pushed Brandon gently into it, letting
him maneuver the board as best he could. The
entire outing took less than a half an hour, and
then Brandon was led back into the villa to
rest. He was such a good kid, Jason thought.
Jason hoped that his father knew what he was
doing. And while Archer was seldom wrong
about anything - in fact Jason had never known
his father to be wrong about anything - Jason
nonetheless held doubts about this stem cell
wonder-cure that his father was so set on.

Jason recalled vividly the arguments
that his mother and father had had over the
issue. His father was always so sure, but there
was something to what his mother said that

just felt right. Mother always said that one had to have faith in the Lord God. She often quoted from Hebrews chapter eleven, verse one. Faith in the Lord, Jason's mother would say, is not something found in any science journal. It's just something you know. Look around you son, evidence of the Lord's existence is everywhere, even within you. Our heavenly father watches over us, in this life and the next.

Talk like this would infuriate Jason's dad. Archer was at best agnostic. "If your God is here, then let him pay for all of the luxuries you enjoy! And why hasn't he healed our son? No, it's me, I'm the one responsible for everything that we have, and I'll be the one to cure our son; not some mythical figure no one can prove has ever existed!"

"But you can't try and cure our son by destroying life! How many children have you murdered? How many more will you destroy? You say this is about our son, but where will it end? You're nothing more than a modern day Doctor Frankenstein! Where will it end? You can't control everything! Stop it! Stop before it's too late!"

That's when Archer would end the conversation. He would punch the wall, throw something, or storm out of the house. This was the part of his dad that made Jason uncertain about him. His Dad always said that he was trying to help Brandon get well. But it seemed that every time his Mom and Dad argued, it ended by his mom saying that Dad was on a quest to rule the world. Jason was well aware of many of his father's holdings, and he also knew of the lab and Doctor Cho. Jason had even met Dr. Cho. His dad had taken Brandon and him to meet Dr. Cho. Dr. Cho had shown the boys his credentials. He wanted them to realize that they were in good hands. Dr. Cho had also taken a biopsy of Brandon's heart. Brandon had spent two weeks in the hospital recovering from that little procedure. Dr. Cho had explained that this was necessary so that the heart that Brandon would receive would be his heart. Jason knew his father worked closely with Doctor Cho. He thought this was because his dad wanted to be sure this time; to do all that he could to ensure that this time Brandon was finally able to live a normal life.

In the back of his mind Jason knew that it was not out of character for his father to want to rule the world, and he was pretty sure that ruling the world had nothing to do with healing his brother, but he was not completely certain. Jason was confused, and his Mother was not around anymore. There were only his father and his brother. Jason loved his father, but he loved his brother even more. His brother needed him, and had always relied upon him. If there was any chance that his father was putting his brother at risk, Jason would be forced do something about it. He was unsure of exactly what he would do, but he knew that he would do whatever it took to make sure that no harm came to Brandon.

****

Archer was back in the lab with Doctor Cho. He wanted to check on the progress of the organs Doctor Cho was cultivating. Archer had just read the latest publication out of Germany. Apparently, the German scientists were asserting that they had obtained stem cells from testes of mice that behaved similarly to the embryonic stem cells that Archer's team used. Doctor Cho was aware of the research, and in fact knew Doctor Lieberman and had discussed the findings only yesterday.

"Well, I don't want us using any sperm cells, especially from any mouse. I like a clean slate. We'll continue to use the embryonic stem cells"

"Yes, of course, Mr. Archer."

"People say I act enough of a prick as it is." Archer laughed heartily at the pun, noting that Doctor Cho did not share his sense of humor. "When will my son's heart be ready?"

"His heart is almost ready Mr. Archer. All we needed was the biopsy of his heart, and we obtained that with his last visit. We have the first of a completed, healthy, vibrant organ, at the proper stage for implementation. I'll need to have your son here first thing Monday morning and, by noon your son will have the first of a completely grown, brand new heart.

"Sunday night we'll be back from the funeral. I'll have him here bright and early. In fact, both of the boys will be with me. I'll need you to reassure them that this will work. Back me up on whatever I say."

"Of course, Mr. Archer."

With that, Archer was gone.

Chapter 14

Thornton's plane had just arrived at the gate. He looked around for Marconi. Would he greet him as he exited the plane? This would not surprise Thornton at all. Marconi had a way of showing up where you least expected him. Thornton had spent time on the plane going over what he would say to Marconi. Thornton remembered that Marconi had told him to take care of Sarah. Marconi had to know that Thornton couldn't take care of anybody, not even himself. At least, Thornton hoped he wouldn't hold him accountable for what that little wench was doing. And what was she doing anyway? Damn her. Things were fine until she came strolling down the hallway that evening. Even worse, she had now accessed his files.

He would tell Marconi that Sarah had snuck into his office while Thornton was away at the funeral. He would explain that Sarah was a threat to them both, someone who could expose them to the police and get them thrown behind bars for a long time. Marconi would be forced to "take care of her" himself. Thornton thought briefly about what might become of Sarah, but told himself that she deserved whatever she got. She should have never come snooping around his office in the first place.

"Ding, ding, ding, ding," the unfastened seatbelt symbol glowed overhead indicating that it was now safe to exit the plane. Everyone stood as if there was a race to see who could get to the baggage claim area first. Thornton stood and filed in line. When he entered the airport he looked about nervously. No Marconi. He breathed a temporary sigh of relief. Once outside he hailed a cab and headed home.

Marconi was sitting outside of Thornton's building, watching and waiting. He waited 30 seconds after Thornton entered the building, hoping to catch him right after he had unlocked his door. The doorman looked up, saw it was Marconi, and nodded his approval. This was not the first time that Marconi had visited Thornton's home. Marconi took the stairs up to Thornton's floor. Upon reaching the floor, he peered through the glass, down the hallway; he could see Thornton exit the elevator. As soon as Thornton unlocked his door, Marconi opened the hall door, just in time to see Thornton's nosey neighbor open her door. She had heard Thornton. She was probably listening for his return.

Thornton also heard the door open, and turned to see the neighbor. Marconi knew he didn't have time to catch Thornton without being seen by this neighbor, who would surely alert Thornton. He stepped back and closed the door slowly, peering through the glass at Thornton. Thornton looked past the neighbor, and saw Marconi peering through the glass. Upon seeing Marconi, Thornton dropped his keys. He was frightened, and visibly shaken. The neighbor turned to see what had startled him, but Marconi was back just far enough so as not to be seen by her. Thornton said a nervous "Hello Ms. Howard."

"Hi Thornton. Where've you been?"

"I was out of town on business." Thornton bent down and picked up his keys.

"I've been watching your place for you."

"Thanks Ms. Howard."

"You had a visitor".

Marconi had moved closer to the door opening it slightly so he could listen to their conversation.

"I did?" Thornton thought the visitor was Marconi.

"She was very pretty, a really nice girl. Not like those others."

Thornton knew right away that it was Sarah. He glanced down the hall at the door and noted that Marconi was listening. He couldn't have hoped for more. "Did she say what she wanted?"

"She asked about your parents. She seemed to think that you were at your mother's funeral. I told her that your mother had passed away a few years ago, and she seemed quite disturbed by this."

"Yes, I think there was a misunderstanding at the office, and she is a very emotional person. Did she say anything else?"

"No, only that she was a lawyer."

"Thank you Ms. Howard."

"Thornton dear, just remember that I am here if you need me. Are you doing alright?"

"Yes Ms. Howard. Thanks for asking." He opened the door and entered his apartment. He thought about locking and chaining the door, but that would only upset Marconi. As soon as he shut the door Ms. Howard closed her door, and Marconi came out of the fire escape. Without knocking, Marconi opened Thornton's door and went in.

"Hello Thornton. Where you been?"

"I needed to get away. Sarah, the attorney I work with, she's out of control. She went into my Office while I was out and I think she looked at the Jackrabbit file. She wanted me to go to the police and tell them everything I know."

"You fool!" Marconi wanted to snap Thornton's neck. This little chippie was quite a piece of work. Focus. "What exactly is in the Jackrabbit file?"

Thornton blurted out, without pause: "It contains the chemical formulas and methods for generating tissue by harvesting stem cells and combining them with host cells to grow organs that the host will accept with almost no chance of rejection."

"Grow organs?"

"Yes".

"You mean like livers and kidneys stuff like that?

"Yes."

"Holy shit!" Marconi knew immediately that he had sold out on the cheap. Archer was planning on making millions, billions. Who wouldn't pay for a new liver? Who wouldn't pay whatever it costs? Damn. Marconi thought for a moment..."How long before anyone actually does this?"

"That depends. Here in the U.S. the laws are such that you can't use aborted fetuses, so the supply of stem cells, the really good ones, is limited. But if you were in a country that allowed that kind of thing, where there were no restrictions on where the stem cells came from, you'd have virtually an unlimited supply of sources and thus cells to work from, and from what I've read we could only be months away from producing the first of these organs.

Marconi knew that Archer's resources were virtually limitless. That bastard!

Marconi couldn't wait to see Archer. The $10,000 Archer had paid Marconi to put the squeeze on Thornton was an insult.

****

Thornton was relieved to see Marconi leave. But he still had one big problem...Sarah. He had hoped that Marconi would take care of Sarah, with all of her meddling. She should never have eavesdropped on him that night in his office. And even now she was still snooping. She had some nerve to come to his home. Well, he had summoned the nerve to confront her once, he could do it again. But not tonight. He was tired. Besides, she might be with that cop friend of hers. First thing in the morning he would go and tell Sarah what he had told Marconi. Getting these two together could only benefit Thornton. One would cancel out the other, Thornton didn't care which, either way was good for him. Although, with Sarah out of the picture, he could go back to the way things were with Marconi. He didn't mind borrowing money, He didn't mind owing money. All that mattered to Thornton was having a good time with money in his pocket and beautiful women at his beckon call.

Chapter 15

The wind blew fiercely, causing the rain to slice across Sarah's face. While most of the onlookers huddled underneath their oversized umbrellas attempting to shield their bodies from the wind and rain, she stood over Jill Archer's gravesite empty handed, certain that the drenching she received was the least she had coming. If only she had called for help…no matter what Jake said, she knew that she was partly to blame for the body now lying here. No way was she going to miss this funeral. What better place to express her guilt and remorse.

The Archers were traditional Catholics, which meant that the service was ceremonial and long. Family and friends from all over the world were in attendance. Archer and the boys remained stoic throughout, not a single tear shed between the three of them. Sarah was sure that Archer had encouraged the boys to put on a good face. He had probably fed them some ridiculous notion about real men never crying, at least not in public. Sarah had cried. She cried for them, for their mother, and for herself. She cried not only for a life tragically taken too soon, but also for a budding relationship that could never bloom. She thought about Jake. She had to make it clear to him that he could not be a part of her life. Not now. He looked so handsome sliding into the pew next to her in the church. It took all of her willpower to get up and move to a pew on the other side of the isle. She would never forget the look on his face. Confusion, disappointment, hurt. He had not followed or tried to approach her since her breaking down in front of him.

As the final prayer was said and the mourners began to disperse, Sarah stood staring off into the distance, oblivious to the chill seamlessly seeping inside her raincoat. At first she didn't feel the slight pressure on her arm. She was so lost in thought that his presence went unnoticed until he positioned himself directly in front of her. Sarah stepped back, and seeing Jason, the sadness increased as she looked up into his eyes. "I'm so sorry for your loss Jason." The cheerful boy that Sarah had met was gone; in his place was a man of sorrow. At that moment he looked much older than his seventeen years.

"Thank you for coming Ms. Davenport. My mother would have wanted you to be here". Jason continued to hold Sarah's arm with his right hand while holding the umbrella over the two of them with his left. "May I speak with you for a moment?" Jason escorted her to a covered shelter a few yards away from the burial site.

"What can I help you with?" Sarah said, as she brushed her wet hair back from her eyes.

"The police report said that you were the last person to speak to my mother before she was murdered, and that you discovered the body. Can you tell me the last thing that she said? Did she speak of me or Brandon?"

Sarah studied his face trying to decide how much information this young man could adequately process at this time. She did not want to convey her suspicions about his father's involvement in his mother's death. He was dealing with enough as it was. "We were discussing some legal documents your mother wanted me to look over for her. I'm not really sure what all they entailed. By the time I arrived at the house she was dead." Sarah watched as Jason lowered his head, visualizing his moms last few minutes of life. "I don't believe she suffered." This time Sarah held his arm. "Your mom was a wonderful lady."

"Do you think the police will catch the person who did this?"

"Yes, I believe they will. Your mother's murderer will not go unpunished."

Jason took a long look at Sarah. He breathed deeply, seemingly in acceptance of events. His mother was gone and he had to move on. He thanked her for her kindness and walked away.

Sarah was just about to head for her car when she spotted a man walking towards the mausoleum on her left. Something about his presence was familiar. She looked once and then again, and fought the urge to dismiss the thought – she knew this man. It was the thug from the park, the one who had kidnapped her and continually threatened her and her sister's life. What was he doing here? Spying on her was the thought that came to mind. However, she quickly dismissed that as she watched his determined strides. No, he was a goon on a mission. One that this time, did not involve her. On impulse she decided to become the pursuer instead of the pursued.

****

"So how come the wife didn't rate a spot inside the family crypt?"

Archer turned to face Marconi as he entered the mausoleum. He resented like hell the note Marconi had slipped to him during the service demanding that he meet him here. "You must be crazy arranging to meet like this. This had better be important." Archer did not raise his voice but was obviously agitated. He pressed down on the back of each finger, systematically cracking his knuckles one by one. "You appear to hold yourself in a higher position than you ought", he said with a sneer.

"Are you forgetting that you work for me? I do the summoning, not the other way around. If you want to keep earning the commission that I'm paying you, then I suggest you remember that."

"And I suggest that you come up with a whole lot more than the piddling amount of cash you've thrown my way."

"You have always been paid in full for your services. I'm not giving you a damn thing more. You greedy, ego-inflated con. How dare you come here and try and shake me down. We have nothing more to discuss. Now leave me alone to mourn my dead wife in peace." Archer glared fiercely, expecting Marconi to retreat.

"I won't be leaving just yet. When I agreed to our original deal I was not privy to all the information I now have. At the time I turned it over to you, I had no idea of how valuable the Jackrabbit project was." Marconi smiled as he watched Archer's expression go from one of smug superiority to a guarded apprehension.

"The Jackrabbit file is no longer your concern. You sold the information to me, and if memory serves, it was you who set the price. I didn't haggle or try to low ball you. I gave you what you asked."

"Well now I'm asking for more. $10,000 is hardly fair when you stand to make millions. I just want a percentage of what I'm due."

Archer knew that this was no time to haggle. "How much more," Archer asked.

Without pause Marconi replied, "Ten Million."

"What makes you think the information is worth that? And even if it is, what makes you think that I'd be willing to pay more for something I already have. You can't unsing the song or play the canary to the police without clipping your own wings." Archer shook his head, "No… you haven't got a leg to stand on and we both know it."

"What I do know is the service industry. I've been providing it for a very long time and I know that people are willing to pay just about anything to get what they want. What I don't know is science or formulas and such, which is why I had no idea what I was selling. You can best believe that, had I known that I was turning over the key to making body parts, I would have certainly held out for a better offer." Marconi shot Archer a wide grin. He continued, "If you don't want to pay and be the sole distributor, then I'm certain I can find someone willing to enter the race with you."

Archer was seething inside. He was not going to let this son-of-a-bitch keep him from achieving his destiny. "I'll give you ten percent now, in cash, and the remainder after the first successful transplant."

One million. Cash. Well that was a nice start to the life that he envisioned for himself. He would agree to take it, knowing that Archer could not be trusted to turn over the rest. Once the process was developed the information would no longer be of value. He had to start shopping for buyers now. The one million would tide him over until he found someone, or several someones willing to pay even more.

The two men didn't shake hands. They gave their word and made arrangements, but neither trusted the other. There was no friendship, no mutual respect, only resentment and deception. They made a pact for now. A pact so paper-thin it was nearly translucent.

****

Sarah stumbled as she approached the opening of the mausoleum. The stones under her feet were slippery from the rain. She stopped and, cautiously, peeked inside, using the outside wall as a barricade to hide most of her body. The man she followed had his back to her, but the other man was facing her, clearly visible. It was John Archer. The revelation that the men knew one another was unsettling. The very two men who had recently caused such turmoil in her life were standing face to face. As the wind blew and the rain continued to fall, Sarah fought the urge to go inside and confront the both of them. It was impossible to hear what they were saying, given her distance from them. She could tell however, from their expression and stance, that it was not a cordial conversation. She continued to observe them without stirring as water trickled from her wet hair. She could have been one of the many figurines that inhabited the cemetery. Her body became so numb it took a moment to realize that the steady pressure on her shoulder was not the fallen rain, but a hand. Inhaling the scream in her throat before it escaped, she raised her head slightly over her right shoulder imagining one of the figurines had come to life. What a wild imagination. She had not conjured up some graveside figurine. She had conjured up Jake.

He crouched down next to her and whispered, "Am I interrupting some clandestine meeting with a corpse"

"Of course not…what are you doing here?"

"I could ask you the same."

Sarah took a deep breath and started to give him what she hoped was a plausible explanation. Nothing came to mind. There was absolutely nothing she could say that would make any sense, except for the truth. "The man inside talking with Archer kidnapped me from my home the first night you were there, threatened my sister's life, and has forbidden me to have anything to do with you." She exhaled. What a relief to have that secret out in the open, off of her chest. Sarah had never been good at deception. In college she was constantly criticized for her inability to keep a poker face. She no longer wanted to keep things from Jake.

He looked at her as if she had suddenly grown horns. If this man had kidnapped her as she claimed then why the hell was she crouched down in the rain spying on him outside of a mausoleum? Jake's grip on her shoulder tightened. "What are you doing here? And why have you not told me this before?"

"I'm not quite sure what I'm doing here. But I do know that I can't go to the police"

"Sarah, in case my badge and job has escaped you, you just did. If you are sure that this guy inside is the one who kidnapped you, then I'll go in and get him." Bracing his hands on his knees he began to rise.

"No! Jake please you can't do that." Sarah reached out tugging him back down. "This man knows where I live, where my sister lives. He has someone following her. I cannot put her life at risk."

"You cannot just expect me to do nothing. I need to at least find out who this man is." Jake could see that she was visibly trembling and knew that it had nothing to do with the cold rain. He was a man of action. He'd been trained to protect the innocent and destroy the threat. Sarah was asking him to ignore that. He attempted to quash his instincts, but just couldn't. "Stay here while I go ask him and Archer some questions." Again he made a move to rise only to be snatched back to the ground with such force that he fell off balance landing on top of Sarah.

"Don't do it. Don't make me regret telling you all of this. To you this is just a job; to me it's my life and the life of my sister."

Jake's hands were positioned on either side of Sarah's body. Upon falling, he had braced himself to avoid crushing her. She looked beautiful lying there in the wet grass beseeching him with her eyes. Maybe she was right. Now was not the time for confrontation. That man could be armed and Sarah could get hurt. Suddenly he heard voices approaching from the opening of the mausoleum. He quickly jumped to his feet, snatching Sarah, they ran to the side of crypt just before Archer and the other man came out. They headed in opposite directions. Jake told Sarah to stay put as he followed the kidnapper at a discrete distance. Jake watched the man as he slid inside an expensive grey sedan. He committed the tag number to memory as it drove down the block.

When Jake returned to Sarah, she was still huddled on the side of the crypt where he had left her. She looked like an abandoned kitten, shivering but sweet. He reached for her hand and wrapped her in his arms and ushered her to his car. Just as he would the kitten, Jake decided to take her in. He'd make arrangements to get her car later, but for now they were heading to his place.

Chapter 16

Jake's place was not what Sarah expected. She'd imagined the stereotypical police detective pad. Small one bedroom apartment, files scattered throughout, leftover Chinese takeout boxes piled up in the trash and a refrigerator with nothing but beer. The reality, however, was far different. Jake's trendy loft was not only spacious, but immaculate. The decor was warm and inviting with large windows that overlooked the bay. Carpet so plush it left the entire imprint of your feet as you walked through it. Immediately upon entering, Jake hit the switch that ignited the huge electric fireplace in the center of the main living room.

"The first thing we need to do is get you out of those wet clothes," Jake said as he assisted her in removing her raincoat. "Make yourself comfortable while I go and get the shower ready." He was also wet and cold, but the look he sent her way was filled with pure heat.

Sarah was suddenly nervous. Was he preparing the shower for them both? Or was she projecting her own desires into what could be a simple act of kindness. She already admitted to herself that she wanted him, and she was fairly certain that he knew it. Then again, she had given him the brush-off on more than one occasion. Maybe his ego would prevent him from trying again, despite her valid reasons for keeping him at bay. Jake returned and ushered her into the bathroom and handed her a bath towel and washcloth. After he left, she discarded her wet clothing and allowed the hot water to work its magic. Get it together Sarah, she thought. She was not used to feeling this uncertain and did not like it one bit. It was time she regained control of her life. Up to now she was always on the defense. No more. In order to win, she would have to mount an offensive attack. She would need to put together a plan of action in order to protect herself and her sister, and get the man she wanted as well.

Jake had left a terrycloth robe on the hook by the shower for her. It was large and warm. She found comfort in wrapping herself in something that belonged to him. Feeling relaxed and refreshed, she found Jake in the kitchen pouring two cups of hot coffee. He too had showered at some unknown location within his house. The robe he wore was identical to the one she was wearing. He must be one of those people who bought items they liked in duplicate, sometimes even triplicate.

Jake immediately took note of Sarah as she entered the kitchen. His robe was nicely bunched around her body. The belt tied tightly around her waist emphasized its small diameter. Bare toes peeped out from beneath the edge of the hem, highlighted by manicured toenails that looked as if they came straight out of an open-toed sandals ad. Her hair was piled high on top of her head, several damp wisps curled endearingly at each temple. The overall effect was too sexy for Jake to resist. He swept her up in his arms and kissed her as he'd wanted to do since she snubbed him in the church earlier. She responded with unbridled enthusiasm. Pleasure was the thought that came to Jake's mind. Pure and simple. The last thing he wanted to do was end this kiss, but that's exactly what he had to do. Reluctantly he stepped back, sliding Sarah's arms from around his neck. "We need to talk sweetheart."

They took their coffee into the living room and sat down on the sofa directly in front of the fire. "Start from the top", Jake said. "Beginning with the moment you first met John Archer."

Sarah recited her history with Archer, once again reliving the horror of his wife's murder. She was more convinced than ever that it had been John Archer who had attacked her in the house. She reiterated this belief to Jake even though she knew he had an alibi.

"Tell me about the kidnapping. Archer had to be involved since he was meeting with the guy who took you."

"I can tell you I was shocked to see the two of them together. I considered the possibility that it had been Archer behind the kidnapping, but then dismissed it as a coincidence."

"I don't believe in coincidences," Jake said. "There has to be a connection. What makes you think that Archer did not hire this guy?"

"Thornton." Sarah let the name drop as if it alone explained all the mysteries of the world including those found inside Pandora's Box.

"Who or what is a Thornton?"

Sarah giggled. His questioned brought to mind a book from her childhood *Horton Hears a Who* by Dr. Seuss. "Thornton Hilliard is an attorney that I work with. He has gotten into some …trouble." Sarah caught her bottom lip between her teeth and began to lightly suck on it. "I'm not sure that I should be discussing the actual issues with a cop, but I will say that Thornton has done something that could not only jeopardize his job, but his freedom as well. Suffice it to say that Thornton acted unethically and, as a result, information was turned over to someone that should not have been. The funny thing is that the guy who kidnapped me did so to ensure my silence, and I'm not exactly sure what it is I'm supposed to remain silent about."

"The night the shot was fired through your window, did he take you then?"

"Yes. After the shot was fired I somehow blacked out and woke up in a dirty warehouse on the west side of town. The man with Archer was there and told me to keep quiet about Thornton's activities. He had a photo of my sister and threatened to harm her if I went to the police." As she spoke, Sarah took note of Jake's change in expression. He looked angry. Really angry.

Jake knew that anger was a futile emotion that blocked all rational thought, but once the seed took root it was hard to contain. He could not believe that Sarah was taken right from beneath his nose; could not believe that he had been right there with her, for goodness sake. According to Sarah, the man had known that he was a cop. In fact, that was supposedly part of the reason he'd come, and yet he came in anyway. This man was methodical and bold. Jake knew the dangers of dealing with someone like this. He had to be on top of his game if he was to be victorious over a person such as him. Jake attempted to clear his mind by drawing on his reserved restraint, and outwardly displayed a calm he didn't feel. "Tell me the rest of it."

"It was he who called the night of our date. He knew that we were together and told me to end it immediately. He told me that I had to stay away from the cops. All cops. He then approached me the next day while I was out running. He made it clear that you were off limits, or else." It was hard to ascertain what Jake was thinking as she told him the story. His face was expressionless.

"How could you not tell me this right away?"

"I couldn't! I wasn't sure what you would do or how you would react."

"You mean you didn't trust me to protect you," Jake blurted out. He rose to his feet and began pacing the room.

"I'm sorry." She began to apologize, and then realized she had nothing to apologize for. What did she really know about him? He acted as if she had somehow challenged his manhood. Men could be so infuriating. She could no longer remain seated on the sofa and rose. As she rose, so too did the pitch of her voice. "Let's get one thing straight detective. I've been looking out for myself for a long time now, and I do not now nor have I ever needed a man to take care of me."

Jake was initially taken-a-back, but inside he smiled, appreciative of her strength. He was not angry at Sarah, and regretted taking his frustrations out on her. It was

153

apparent to him that she felt strongly about her independence. He walked over to Sarah and held out his hand. He flashed his most appealing smile. "Please, let's sit back down and finish talking."

Sarah grabbed his palm and allowed him to lead her back to the sofa. They sat in silence for only a minute, but it seemed more like twenty. Jake finished his coffee while Sarah stared at the glowing flames in the fireplace. She wanted Jakes help. Maybe even needed it. Finally Sarah said, by way of explanation, "The last man in my life tried to mold me into his version of what he thought a woman should be. At first I thought that Derek was the most wonderful man in the world. The initial changes he made in my life seemed harmless, even sweet, until I realized that what he wanted was someone different from me. We'd go shopping and he'd pick out my outfits. I felt fortunate to have a man who was not only willing to shop, but actually seemed to enjoy shopping. Before long my entire wardrobe had become something, to use Derek's words, more appropriate to wear. Derek would take me on these fabulous trips and even make arrangements with my boss to lighten my case load so that we could be away for extended periods. But his ultimate goal was to get me to quit my job so I'd be totally dependent upon him. Barefoot and pregnant was Derek's idea of the perfect wife."

"He's an idiot" Jake said, looking her strait in the eyes. "I'd take a feisty independent woman over a helpless homebody any day."

"This from a guy who can't commit," Sarah teased. Jake had already told her about his ex-girlfriend Melanie and how their relationship ended because she'd wanted to be a wife.

"It's not that I can't commit" Jake said. "I simply choose to reserve my commitment for the right woman."

For a moment Sarah wished that she could be that woman. "Hey I've got a great idea. Why don't we introduce our exes? They sound perfectly suited for one another."

Jake laughed out loud imagining the irony of that scenario. "About as perfect as the two of us" he said as he continued to chuckle.

Sarah's smile faded. "What are you trying to say?"

"That I know we'd be good together." Jake replied.

"How do you know?" Sarah asked, hoping for the right answer.

"I know because I've thought of little else since we met. How can you doubt the connection between us? If not for that untimely phone call the other night, we would have had sex in my car like some hormonal teenagers."

Good answer. Sarah wanted to deny it but… she wanted him, and she knew that he knew that she wanted him.

He approached her. "Allow me to convince you." The kiss, finally coming, was electric. He cradled her head in his hands, bunching masses of her hair in his fists. The intensity between them made her want to get even closer. Something hot and achy started to spark between them. The passion grew so fierce that they soon lost all control. Robes came undone. Arms and legs intertwined. Bodies fell to the carpet.

Tonight they would shut out the world and all its problems. Tomorrow they would deal with whatever came along, together. For the second time that day Sarah gave into her instincts and trusted this man. The first time she risked her life. This time - her heart.

Chapter 17

First thing Monday morning, Archer brought the boys to Dr. Cho's office. There, using a model heart, Dr. Cho explained to Jason and Brandon how Brandon's new heart would work. Dr. Cho was very patient. He explained that their dad had sought him for his expertise in this area. He assured the boys that he had personally worked to ensure that this was as safe as any procedure available, and that he had used all of his knowledge and experience to "build" Brandon a heart constructed just for him. He told Brandon that all he had needed to make Brandon's new heart was the sample he had taken from Brandon months ago, and now his new heart was ready.

Jason listened to Dr. Cho and watched Brandon's eyes light up. He too was becoming excited at the prospect of his little brother finally becoming normal. In the back of his mind, however, he wondered exactly how Dr. Cho had built Brandon's heart. He wondered if there were children who were sacrificed so that his brother could have his new heart, and if so, how many?

"Do you have any questions?" Dr. Cho asked, breaking Jason away from his thoughts.

"Will it hurt?" Brandon asked?

"Well, there will be a little discomfort," Dr. Cho replied, "but we will put you to sleep and when you wake up, it'll all be over. You'll have to rest here for a few days after the operation, but this should be the last operation you'll ever need."

Brandon looked at Jason, who smiled a genuine smile. Brandon was comforted. He said "O.K. I'm ready." Brandon stood and went off with Dr. Cho.

Archer turned to Jason and told him that this would be a long morning, so he should make himself comfortable. Archer then followed Dr. Cho and Brandon into the hallway, leaving Jason in the office. He meandered over to the door, and peering through the window, he saw two women entering through the clinic doors. One of the women was pregnant. His facial expression turned to one of curiosity. He then headed out into the hallway to see where the ladies were going.

Jason soon caught up to the two women and followed them for several minutes, more because the women were moving so slowly, not because they had a long distance to travel. Down the hallway and a right turn down another hallway, and then to the left into a large waiting area where several other women were seated. Jason kind of peaked around the corner so as not to be seen by the nurses/receptionists behind the station. He stood out. There were only medical personnel dressed in white jackets or blue uniforms or ugly green scrubs, or indigenous, women in this place.

From the waiting room there appeared to be a hallway leading away from where Jason was standing. Emerging from the hallway was a man dressed in white pants and coat, holding a clipboard. He came into the waiting area and, looking down at the clipboard, called out for a Magdalena Esposito Alonzo. Jason saw a woman look up at the man, and rise from her seat rather gently. Funny, he thought, she didn't appear to be pregnant. Jason decided to slip past the waiting area and see what else was going on in this place. He put his head down and walked firmly past the waiting area, continuing down the hallway.

Jason came upon a hallway that was dimly lit - odd for the otherwise bright building. There were two men, boys really, about Jason's age, who were pushing a large bin opposite his direction. The way they were dressed led Jason to believe that they were a couple of orderlies, except that they were wearing masks to cover their nose and mouth. They turned to the right and disappeared. Jason followed down the hallway. Near the end of the hallway there was a set of double doors to the right, and above the doors where the boys had turned down was a sign marked "Medical Waste." Jason pushed through one of the doors and he could hear the boys laughing and joking in the distance. He also, for the first time, noticed an odor in the air. It was a foreign odor; a smell he had not, before now, experienced. There was formaldehyde, but there was something else, an animal odor, but one that sent a chill through his body. He followed. There, a few steps into the hallway was an opening on the left. The boys were emptying the bin into some sort of huge metallic underground tank.

Jason inched towards the boys, and towards the edge of the tank. As he got closer, what he saw made him sick to his stomach. Babies. Deformed, no, half-formed babies. Almost alien looking. Some so small you couldn't even make out that they were human, except that they were all mixed in together with bigger, more formed fetuses. Jason convulsed, and heaved, and vomited. The boys who were emptying the bin into the tank turned at the sound of Jason's heaving. They were startled, wide-eyed at first, but one of the boys quickly yelled something to Jason in Spanish. Jason tried to back away, but stumbled. The other boy ran over and put a hand on Jason's shoulder and asked with a heavy Hispanic accent, "hey, are ju O.K.?"

Jason coughed and breathed deeply, and composed himself for a moment. He said he was fine, and just then he realized that he was smelling the odor of dead human flesh, and he bent over and vomited again.

Ortega, the boy who was standing near Jason, pulled off his gloves and set them to the side. He walked Jason through the back of the room and outside. The sun was bright. The air clean. The other boy followed. Outside in the fresh air Jason recovered. The boys explained to Jason what the facility was and what went on there. They explained the abortions, and they also talked about discarding eggs that Jason assumed were not viable for use for in-vitro fertilization.

They thought Doctor Cho was a mad scientist. Ortega was the first to discover the laboratory where the organs were grown. He had shown the lab to Juan. Neither had access to the area, but working there, one heard rumors and stories of the goings-on there, and both had known women who had used the clinic for abortions. Despite the heavily catholic population, abortions were an accepted part of what went on in the local community, even if it went unspoken. Besides, it was hard to pass up the money that was offered.

"Si. They offer the money for the abortions, and the sooner you have the

abortion, the more money you will get."
Ortega said he and Juan were fortunate to have their jobs. Working here was about the best job around on the island.

The boys explained to Jason that a lot of the eggs and the very under developed fetuses, or what was left of them, came from the area where Doctor Cho's laboratory was located. It wasn't hard for Jason to figure out the connection between stem cells and what Doctor Cho was doing, and it turned his stomach into knots. He loved his brother and wanted him to be well, but at what cost? Was it right that his brother have a new heart if it cost the life, or lives of unborn children, just because his father was able to afford to give Brandon a new heart? Jason thanked Ortega and Juan, and headed off to find his father and brother.

Chapter 18

Sarah awakened the next morning in Jake's arms. Both were early risers. Both had a lot on their minds. Jake was eager to find out about Marconi... and Thornton. Sarah, sensing that Jake was awake, and anticipating his eagerness, said "After breakfast, let's track down Thornton." Jake responded with a smile she could feel and a gentle kiss in her ear, and then whispered that they grab breakfast on the way to Thornton's. "We won't get anywhere if you keep that up." Sarah said.

They arrived at Thornton's place just after 8 o'clock in the morning. Thornton was still having coffee when Sarah knocked on his door. The knock was gentle, and Thornton thought it was Ms. Mednick from down the hall. He opened the door, still in his robe, and said "Yes Ms. Medni..." Upon seeing Sarah and Jake he tried to close the door, but Jake put his size 12 loafers at the base of the door and stopped it, then sidestepped Sarah and pushed the door and Thornton backwards. Before Thornton could say a word Jake had his badge in Thornton's face and was reading him his rights. Thornton was shocked. His mind was racing. He first thoughts were that he was going to prison for the Jackrabbit patent. His next thoughts were that Marconi was going to kill him. He began to cry.

Jake cast a glance at Sarah, and they both shared a sly smile. "Sit down." Jake said after reading Thornton his rights. If you cooperate, I can promise you it'll go a lot easier on you. Thornton wept louder. Sarah came over and put her hand on Thornton's shoulder. Thornton jerked away. Jake said "All we want is Marconi." This got Thornton's attention. He looked up at Jake and wiped the tears and snot from his face. Sarah handed him a tissue. "Marconi?" Thornton repeated, looking up at them both. "Yes." Jake said. "We know he's behind the whole thing." Thornton began weeping again, only this time it was out of a feeling of relief. "We need you to tell us everything."

Thornton started from the beginning, when he met Marconi in a Gentleman's club almost a year ago. Thornton told them about the loans, the trips, and eventually the patent. Thornton even told them about their meeting two days ago, and how interested Marconi became after learning about the patent application, and what it did.

"So let me get this straight," Jake said, "Marconi had you deliver him the patent without knowing what it was about?" "That's correct," Thornton replied.

"And that was two days ago." Jake said, looking over at Sarah. They were both thinking the same thing: Marconi shows up at Mrs. Archer's funeral to meet with Archer the day after learning about this patent.

"I'm going to need you to repeat this story down at the station," Jake said. Terror returned to Thornton's eyes. Jake said "Look Thornton, I am not placing you under arrest, I am taking you down to the station so that you can give us a statement. If you cooperate, I'll do all that I can to keep you out of jail. Now get dressed and let's go." Sarah and Jake turned to each other and each said to each other at the same time: "We need to talk to Archer." Thornton returned and they all headed down to the station.

****

Dr. Cho came into the waiting room both relieved and pleased. He was relieved because his most precious patient had received an unprecedented heart transplant of what was, in large part, his own heart. He was doing exceptionally well. So much so that his recovery time would be much shorter than even Dr. Cho had originally anticipated. The look on his face told the story even before he could utter a word to Archer and Jason. When Archer heard the news his mind was racing. He was euphoric, and for many reasons. Jason was also happy, so happy he felt a tear form in the corner of his eye. He quickly turned to the side and with both hands rubbed his face so as to remove the tear without being noticed. He wished his mother was alive.

Archer told Dr. Cho to prepare for the next phase. Dr. Cho understood this to mean that Archer wanted the same operation. Jason also heard this, and his thoughts turned to the bin of dead children. He wondered how far his dad would go in harvesting embryos and aborted fetuses. He wondered what the next phase entailed.

Archer said to Dr. Cho "When can we see Brandon?" Hearing this brought Jason back to the here and now. "We should let him rest, but in the morning he should be well enough for a brief visit. Besides, it will do him well to see you both."

Archer's phone vibrated, and he put the phone to his ear. It was his office calling. A Detective Reed had called for him. He left a message that he wanted to speak with Archer. He must have some information on Jill, Archer thought. "Tell him we can speak tomorrow afternoon. I'll be back around one."

Jason asked if they could at least see Brandon, and they all headed off to the recovery room.

****

The next afternoon Archer was back in the U.S. His car met him on the runway and off

166

he went to his office. On the way he phoned Jake and said they could meet in his office at two.

Jake was ready. Sarah had searched Archer's business ventures and discovered an obscure medical laboratory in Korea, specializing rather vaguely in medical research. There were also subsidiaries in Southeast Asia and one in the Caribbean. Sarah and Jake had discussed her findings over breakfast, and while Sarah had fought to attend the meeting with Archer, Jake felt her presence would complicate matters. Sarah agreed, almost too easily, and had, unbeknownst to Jake, made an airline reservation to an Island in the Caribbean, to visit a medical clinic.

The plane landed smoothly enough. The sky was tattered with low hanging thin white clouds in the forefront, and the clear blue sky as the background. A warm breeze blew across Sarah's face as she walked down the stairs that had been wheeled over to the plane. Inside the terminal fans circulated warm air, and a band greeted the travelers with smooth Latin sounds. Once outside, Sarah agreed to one of the many taxi drivers who approached her, and was on her way directly to the clinic.

****

"Mr. Archer, how are you?"

"Fine." Archer replied rather abruptly. There was no love lost between these two. "Have you any news on who murdered my wife?"

"We're pursuing a couple of leads, but nothing concrete."

"Well then what's this about? You public servants sure have a way of taking your time about things. Nothing works like capitalism. Money. The almighty dollar, that's what…"

Jake cut him off. "I'm looking for Marconi."

Jake studied Archer's face as he said this, knowing that this moment was crucial to the truth, regardless of what Archer said.

It had the desired effect. Archer was hit in the face with the question. A stinging blow. But like an experienced boxer he stepped back and gathered himself. This detective knew of Marconi, but what did he know? Archer couldn't be sure. His first instinct was to end the meeting and tell this pompous public servant that any more questions would have to go through his lawyer. But that would be admitting defeat. No. This "detective" was no match for Archer. He could spar with the best of them.

Archer decided to acknowledge Marconi. Even better, he could put this detective onto Marconi. Throw Marconi under the bus. Hopefully eliminate Marconi. As useful as he had been, men like him were a dime a dozen. So Archer would get to Marconi and his blackmail, but first see what this Detective was willing to divulge.

"Do you mind if I ask why you are looking for Marconi?"

"So you admit you know the man." Jake was seasoned and knew it was best to answer a question with a question.

"Yes, I know him. I've hired Marconi to do an odd job for me here and there. Unfortunately the relationship soured." Archer was smiling inside.

"How so?" Jake asked.

"Well, the last time I saw him he was trying to blackmail me for a lot of money…ten million dollars." Archer thought it best to get ahead of the story. "In fact I'm supposed to meet with him and bring a down payment, if you will. He threatened to harm my sons. How do you know this?"

"I didn't." Jake replied. Jake knew of the story Thornton had told, and he was taking Archer's story with a grain of salt. This could be why Marconi was at the funeral, but Jake wasn't quite ready to let the Jackrabbit patent go just yet. Focus, Jake told himself. "You say Marconi was hired for the occasional odd job, could you elaborate?"

"Well, most of the few jobs I had for him were done out of the country. I'm sure you would have no interest in them."

"Humor me." Jake replied.

"Look Detective, I just told you the man is trying to blackmail me. It would seem to me that you should be doing some of that protecting and serving right about now instead of questioning me about why I hired Marconi for some overseas work!"

Jake sensed he was onto something.

"Well Archer," the mister Archer was gone now, "I'm trying to figure out your interest patents."

Archer flinched, his eyes darted from side to side, but just as quickly he recovered. "I have several companies and intellectual property comprises a large part of our revenue stream, Detective."

"Yes," Jake quickly interjected, "I'm aware of your interest in medical research."

Again Archer flinched, this time even more briefly, and the retreat was replaced by a rising anger. What exactly did this detective know? He decided to ask, "What is it you're trying to get at, Detective?"

I'm simply asking if you know where I can find Marconi? I have information that you and Marconi are both interested in medical research patents, and now you tell me that he's trying to blackmail you and has threatened your family. He sounds like someone we need to get off of the street. I would appreciate your help, and it sounds as if we could help each other." Now it was Jake's turn to smile inside.

Archer knew he needed to cooperate with this guy, and was now calculating the risk of Marconi getting caught and telling everything. He knew that with Marconi's past criminal record that whatever Marconi said against Archer would be suspect. Archer was figuring that all he needed to do was to get Marconi on tape for extortion and whatever he said after that would be to save himself from the three-strikes law. Archer had very good attorneys and had lined the pockets of many local officials. With this he saw the solution to a big problem.

"Look Detective, this Marconi approached me offering to sell me a patent. It wasn't even a patent yet. I refused. As I said, I've had Marconi work for me in the past, so he has some familiarity with my businesses, and he thought he had some brilliant idea for which I would pay him quite handsomely. He asked me for 10 million. I thought he was joking. When I laughed, he became angry. He said something to the effect that nobody laughs at him. The next thing I know he shows up at my wife's funeral threatening my children and blackmailing me. Now Detective, I am usually one to handle my own business, but when it

comes to my children, they're all I have left."
So I agreed to his demand. Archer was back to
smiling inside. The story sounded plausible.

"How is the payment to be made?" Jake
asked.

"We're supposed to meet tomorrow. I
told him that I could only come up with one
million in cash right now. He agreed to that as
a sort of down payment."

Not a lot of time, Jake thought. But he
had to go with it. He couldn't let this
opportunity pass. "Let's set it up. We'll be
there." Jake was satisfied for the moment.

"Thanks." Archer was still smiling
inside.

■■■

Chapter 19

Sarah arrived at the clinic mid-day. On the way over she figured she would pose as an investigative reported for the Post-Daily, and walk right in and ask for Archer. She figured that, that way she would get to speak with whoever was in charge, as they were sure to know Archer.

She approached the counter and, as planned, asked for Mr. John Archer. She identified herself as a reporter, and was initially dismayed to learn that the receptionist had never heard of Mr. Archer. Sarah asked for the Director.

After about five minutes, Dr. Cho entered the reception area and introduced himself. Sarah explained that she was looking for Mr. Archer to interview him on the groundbreaking work with organ reproduction. Sarah said that Mr. Archer had invited her here to see first-hand the progress that had been made. Dr. Cho beamed. While he was aware of the nefarious nature with which the Jackrabbit information had been obtained, he saw this as an opportunity to espouse his own progress. He was more than happy to give Sarah a tour of the facility, albeit a limited tour. Dr. Cho was no fool. He was, however, a proud, and more than a little egotistical scientist, eager to have his work and himself recognized. He explained to Sarah in layperson terms that organ reproduction was an ultimate goal, and that stem cell research was the key. He reminded Sarah that considerable funding was required, but here, unlike other places, the government was in favor of the research, and even encouraged women who had decided to terminate their pregnancies, to "do some good with the children." Sarah was seething behind the smile. This place was sick. The thought repeated itself over and over as Dr. Cho continued to brag about the "good" he was allowed to do here at the facility.

Sarah needed to know if Dr. Cho was aware of Jackrabbit. "So what you're doing here sounds a lot like what they're doing over at Jackrabbit." Dr. Cho was completely taken-a-back. He stopped dead in his tracks, and looked over his horn-rimmed glasses at Sarah as if she had grown horns. "I'm sorry but I cannot speak to you any longer. This meeting is over." With that he turned and walked away.

Sarah decided to give it one last try: "We know about Jackrabbit, Doctor." Dr. Cho stopped and turned back towards Sarah briefly, and realizing that he had said too much already, turned back and proceeded down the hall and out of sight. Sarah turned and headed back towards the entrance.

"Sarah?" Sarah turned. It was Jason. This was better than finding Archer. "Hi Jason. What are you doing here?"

"I'm here with my brother. He just received a brand new heart, grown just for him." Jason was smiling.

"Grown?!?!?" Sarah said.

"Yes!" Jason replied. "Dr. Cho has been working on this for months. He finally got everything he needed and grew Brandon a heart, and just yesterday he implanted Brandon's heart. He said everything went great. I even spoke to Brandon earlier this morning. It was only for a short while, but I think this time he's going to be alright."

Sarah wondered if Dr. Cho finally getting what he needed meant the Jackrabbit patent. "I was just speaking with Dr. Cho. He said his work was fascinating, but he had to run off before he could show me any of his work. You wouldn't know where I could take a look at what he's doing here, would you?"

"Sure. C'mon." Sarah was speechless. Jason showed her the room with all of the hearts in their different stages of development. She could hardly believe her eyes.

"My Dad says that what we're doing here will help a lot of people."

"And what do you think?" Sarah asked. "I can see how this will help. There are a lot of sick people in the world."

Sensing hesitation, Sarah asked "And what do you think?"

"Well…it's just that my Mom…I mean, I don't think my Mom would have approved."

"Why not?" Sarah asked.

"I saw these two guys, Ortega and Juan, and they showed me where all the dead babies are thrown away. It made me pretty sick," Jason said as his voice trailed off.

"Oh, I see," Sarah said. "I kind of think my Mom was right about killing one thing to save another. I don't think it's right either, but my brother has a brand new heart, and I am really happy about that. I don't know. I just don't know."

"Well let's just think about Brandon for now. There will be plenty of time to think about the other stuff later. You said you spoke to Brandon this morning?"

Jason brightened. "Yes. And he's doing pretty good. Dr. Cho said to give him a few weeks and he'll be out swimming the ocean with me. I can't wait."

"Have you eaten?" Sarah asked. "No, not really," Jason replied."

Sarah suggested that they grab a bite. "I have to head back to the States this evening."

"O.K." Jason said, and they were off.

****

By the time Sarah landed, Jake had left her a voicemail. They met for dinner and had a lot to say to each other. They were convinced that Archer had obtained the Jackrabbit patent from Marconi, but couldn't prove it just yet. Once they had Marconi in custody they would hopefully learn much more. Marconi was a lifelong criminal and could prove difficult to work with. On the other hand, he could be the type that would sell his soul to save his ass. And there was probably no love lost between him and Archer.

After dinner Jake went back to Headquarters to put together the finishing touches on the sting they would set-up for Marconi. All he needed Archer to do was to get them together in the same place, with the money. Archer had refused to wear a wire, so rifle microphone would have to suffice. Jake thought of Sarah. They made a good team. He called her. She answered the phone with a raspy, sexy voice that said he had awakened her. He missed her, and he told her. She invited him over, but he said he needed to work and it might be best if he slept in his own bed tonight. He knew it wasn't quite true, but even now he was still a little standoffish. They hung up and Sarah quickly returned to sleep.

The next day came and all was in place. Two shotgun microphones were all that were feasible given the logistics. The meeting was set at the park; late morning. There were a few people around, but soon the lunch crowd would appear. Archer carried a large black leather bag. The bag was filled with one-hundred $10,000 bundles of cash.

There were six undercover officers immediately on the scene; two women ending their jog, one bending over to catch her breath. Another female officer was slowly walking a stroller with a baby doll and a shotgun microphone pointed towards Archer. Opposite her was a male officer dressed as a homeless man lying on a bench. Under the newspapers that covered him was another shotgun microphone pointing at Archer, who was standing a few feet from the bench. Two officers were dressed as young street punks talking loudly about the game last night. Jake was in radio communication with them all, about a quarter of a mile away in an undercover van. Jake's only lament was that they couldn't get a camera at the site.

Marconi arrived on-time. The last thing he suspected was that Archer would have involved the police. Marconi knew too much about Archer's nefarious activities. And seeing the leather bag excited Marconi. He was distracted.

Marconi looked from side to side more from habit than anything else. His gaze quickly returned to the bag, then to Archer. He couldn't help but smile. Archer returned his smile with a sneer. He knew he needed to appear angry. To show the satisfaction that he was feeling inside would alert Marconi that something was afoot.

Marconi spoke first. "When do I get the rest?"

"I'm making arrangements now. Not more than a week," Archer replied.

The two men were face to face. Marconi was eager. He reached out and almost snatched the bag from Archer. Archer pulled back. Marconi's eyes narrowed. Archer, smiling inside, eased the bag over to Marconi. "Don't you want to count it?" Archer asked. Marconi looked around. "Let's walk." Archer knew the set-up and needed to keep Marconi in range of the microphones and the police just long enough to incriminate himself. After that, Archer would wait to see if an opportunity presented itself for the other part of his plan.

Archer also knew that he didn't want Marconi to say too much, lest he mention Jackrabbit. It was a thin line, but if Archer could pull it off, he would be free.

Archer stopped. "Wait a minute you bastard. I just handed you a million dollars. I need a guarantee that after you get the rest, this will be over."

"First things first." Marconi said. "Come with me while I take a quick count of the insides of this bag."

The two walked off the path towards the cover of trees. They were out of sight. Neither said a word. After about twenty feet they stopped. Archer expected Marconi would at least want to look inside the bag. Trust was not one of his stronger qualities.

The detectives didn't expect this, but they couldn't move too quickly to follow lest they be discovered. They all looked at each other. Someone had to follow, but who? Moments passed. The detective on the bench radioed Jake.

Marconi opened the bag and smiled a wide grin. Archer knew it was now or never. He then did something unexpected. With his left hand he reached for the bag of money and pulled. The move startled Marconi, who was not about to let a million dollars get away from him now. He pulled back with two hands.

Archer knew this was it. He let go of the bag and reached inside his pocket with his right hand for the revolver. Marconi saw Archer reaching inside of his jacket, and realized he was reaching for a gun. He had been caught off-guard.

"You son-of-a-bitch!" Marconi's eyes opened wide with astonishment. Marconi was confused. Grab the money or reach for his gun. He tried to do both, and did neither effectively. Archer leveled the weapon and aimed, waiting for the instant when Marconi had his gun in his hand. As soon as Marconi had the weapon in hand, and before Marconi could bring the weapon to bear, Archer fired into Marconi's chest. Once. Marconi's gun hand continued to rise. Twice. Marconi's eyes went from anger to bewilderment. And then a third time. Marconi's eyes rolled in his head. He fell to the ground, his one hand still gripping the bag of cash. The whole thing lasted less than a minute.

The officers were all converging on the scene, weapons drawn." Drop the weapon! Get on the ground!"

Archer immediately held his hands in the air, allowing the revolver to drop along the way, and dropped to his knees.

The first officer on the scene kicked the weapon away and cuffed Archer. The second officer placed a foot on Marconi's gun hand and knelt down and checked Marconi for a pulse. Jake was screaming loudly asking what the hell just happened.

The other officers were standing at the scene, trying to piece together what had happened. Jake was disgusted. He knew now that he should have frisked Archer before the meet. He hadn't.

■■

Chapter 20

As for Archer, his story was sound. They walked away and as they stopped at the trees, Marconi said that this would be over when he said it was over. Archer then reached for the bag, saying that that was not the deal, and when he did Marconi drew his weapon. Archer, knowing Marconi's reputation for violence, had brought his own weapon. One that he had a permit to carry. In his defense, he pulled his weapon and fired. The first shot did not stop Marconi, so he fired two more shots. He was afraid for his life, and the life of his children. The story was partially true, and partially believable. It was just so damned convenient.

****

In the days and weeks that followed, Jake would listen over and over to the exchange between the two men. There was simply not enough there to contradict anything Archer had said.

Jake knew that no jury in the world would convict Archer. Especially given Marconi's criminal history, which Archer's team of attorneys were sure to bring into evidence. Without Marconi, there was no way to connect Archer to the patent. The offshore clinic was outside of Jake's jurisdiction. Jake couldn't touch him. The only thing that remained was to figure out who killed Mrs. Archer. Eric had not turned up any workable clues. Archer was inferring that it could have been Marconi. Sarah was not convinced.

****

Back on the island Brandon's recovery was progressing beyond anyone's wildest expectations. Jason spent all of his time with Brandon. As the weeks and months passed, Brandon was growing bigger and stronger. Even Archer was appreciating that Brandon was beginning to look like an Archer.

****

Sarah was back at work. A couple of months had passed since Archer's shooting. She and Jake had tried to keep seeing each other, but Jake somehow had become more distant, more standoffish.

****

Thornton was given five years of probation, and had been dis-barred. The last Sarah had heard of Thornton was that he was working as a paralegal in a law firm on the other side of town.

****

Sarah was working on another nasty divorce. This time the wife had taken the children out of the state, through her attorney she was alleging that the husband was abusive and did not deserve to be around the children. She had asked the court to mandate supervised visitation. The children were always caught in the middle. Sarah represented the husband, Richard Tully. As she listened to the husband her thoughts again turned to Mrs. Archer. She couldn't help but recall the events of the night Mrs. Archer was found murdered. She recalled vividly the scene. Ringing the front doorbell. Knocking. Finally walking over to the window and seeing Mrs. Archer lying there, lifeless. She remembered going back and trying the door, and when it opened, she recalled the chill that went through her body. She could see it as if it was yesterday. The hallway, and the shadow of the figure that approached her from behind and struck her on the head. It was a man, a big man. Much taller than Marconi. It was Archer. She knew it. She tried to think. What was Archer's alibi? He was here at the firm dropping off financial papers. She had read Chester's affidavit. Chester was sure Archer was there, and had the log to back him up. Chester had no reason to lie. He had been security for the firm for at least as long as Sarah was there. Had Archer paid Chester off?

Ms. Davenport? It was Sarah's new client, trying to bring Sarah back from her thoughts. "I'm sorry Mr. Tully. I'll file the papers with the court first thing in the morning, holding your wife in contempt." Sarah stood to indicate that the meeting was over. "That's all we can do for now. We know where your wife and the children are, and the court will sort this all out." Sarah started moving towards the door, and Mr. Tully took the cue and followed. Sarah opened the door. "Don't worry, we'll get the kids back. I'll call you as soon as I hear from the court."

Sarah walked Mr. Tully to the elevator. As soon as he was on the elevator, Sarah pushed the button and took the next one down. There was Chester. "Hi Chester. I was hoping I could ask you a couple of questions about Mr. Archer. Do you recall the affidavit you filled out?

"Yes Ma'am. Sure do."

"You said that Mr. Archer was here to drop off some papers."

"Sure did."

"What did you think of Mr. Archer?"

Didn't think nothin'. He looked a little rough around the edges."

"Rough around the edges?'

"Yeah. He seemed like the kinda dude you don't wanna mess with."

Well, that was certainly Archer, Sarah thought. Maybe not rough around the edges, but someone you wouldn't want to mess with. But… he wasn't rough around the edges. He was polished. Manicured, every detail neatly in place. Sarah pressed Chester. "Was he a big man?

"He was big alright. Had a neck the size of a tree trunk."

Hmmm. Sarah thought. Sounding more like Marconi. "How tall was he? Was he my height?

"No, shorter than you."

Sarah's adrenalin started pumping. It felt as if she was nearing the finish line after a long race…in first place.

"If I showed you a picture, do you think you could point him out?"

"Of course. A guy like that is hard to forget."

"I'll have to get the picture. I'll be back. Thanks Chester."

"Anytime."

****

●●●

Sarah headed back upstairs and phoned Jake. She told him about her conversation with Chester, and that he needed to bring over a book of mug shots that included Marconi so that Chester could point him out. She was certain that it was Marconi, and not Archer that had come to the firm that evening. If true, Archer no longer had an alibi. Jake suggested bringing Chester to the station where they could make a record of the identification. Archer's lawyers would carve them into pieces with an identification at the lobby of the firm. Sarah agreed. She wasn't a criminal lawyer. Jake sounded excited. Sarah hoped that at least part of that excitement was a result of her calling.

At the station Chester was handled with kid-gloves. He was given coffee, which he preferred black with sugar, just like he preferred his women, he said with a chuckle. And he was given a cushioned chair. The book included photos of Archer and Marconi. It was a head shot only, and seemed to fit in with the mish-mash collection of the myriad crooks, criminals and miscreants.

"Yep, that's him. Right there. I'd remember that face anywhere. Look at that neck. Oooh." Chester shivered a little as he pointed to the picture of Marconi. "Yep, that's him."

Jake and Sarah looked at each other and smiled. "Alright Chester. You can go now. We may need you to repeat what you just did in court one day soon." Jake said.

"No problem. Just let me know when. As long as you pay me for any work I miss. No problem. See you Miss Sarah."

"Thanks Chester. See you back at the office."

****

When they brought Archer in he was again furious. "Get my lawyer. I have nothing to say to you." Of course he had plenty to say. "Where's the Chief? Call the Mayor. When I'm done with you, you'll be lucky to get a job as a crossing guard! You two-bit cop."

The trial lasted a week, with Judge Clarke presiding. Archer's team of lawyers had a team of the best expert witnesses that money could buy. They testified on everything from the time of death to where the murder occurred. Everything Archer's experts testified to contradicted everything the state's witnesses testified to, and Archer's experts did it all with much more flair. It was all smoke and mirrors, designed to cast doubt in the minds of at least one juror. But it was Chester who suffered the most.

As it turned out, Chester had, in the past, broken the law. Chester was cited for speeding 25 years ago and had not paid the ticket, because he simply did not have the money. About a year after receiving the ticket, Chester was driving along, minding his business, and an Officer pulled behind him and ran his tags, probably for no other reason than that Chester was a black man. Chester was arrested on the bench warrant that issued from failing to pay the ticket, and spent a couple of hours behind bars, until his wife, borrowing money from her sister, came and paid the fine. Chester had forgotten all about the arrest. But a team of lawyers with a team of lawyers and a team of researchers could find out any and everything about a person. And when Chester was asked if he had ever been arrested, and said no, poor Chester was made out to be a bigger criminal than Archer and Marconi could ever hope to have been. Most of the jurors seemed sympathetic, but it only takes one to have a hung jury.

It worked. The trial ended in a hung jury.

The prosecutor was hesitant to retry the case, and the Mayor and the Chief were lukewarm at best. But the trial had generated a lot of media attention. Mrs. Archer was quite the philanthropist, and with her connections in the religious community, there was a lot of pressure from outside of the local establishment.

The second trial also ended in a hung jury, and this time the prosecutor was finished with the case. He wouldn't retry it. It was simply too expensive. Besides, almost two years had passed since the murder and the public had lost interest. John Archer was a free man.

During the course of the trial, Jason and Brandon had become distant towards their father, even suspecting that he had possibly had a hand in the murder of their mother. Brandon would be 18 soon. Jason, now 20, had moved out of the house. Archer had not cut him off financially - not yet, but the threat was ever-present.

At one point Jason had asked Sarah whether she thought Archer had murdered his mother. Sarah looked Jason in the eyes and said that she didn't know. She really didn't know for sure, although she suspected that he had.

As for Sarah, she went back to the firm. She finally made partner. There were other clients and more money. As for Jake, they promised each other that they would keep in touch, but days turned into weeks turned into months. Sarah was back to running. This afternoon the sun was shining brightly. She slipped on her ipod and put on an old Frank Sinatra tune, and off she went. Life was good.

Archer was meeting with Dr. Cho. They were finalizing plans for his new heart. The first of what would be many new, improved organs. Archer smiled the smile of a man who had found the key to life itself.